"Look. I just wanted you to know that Melissa and I are over," Ken blurted out.

Maria's eyebrows shot up. "Why are you telling *me* this?" she asked.

Ken blinked. Why wouldn't he tell her? Who else even mattered?

"Because, Maria, I did some crazy, stupid stuff," he explained. "And I want you to know it's all done now. I never really wanted to be with Melissa anyway. I only felt sorry for her after everything that happened with Will." He paused, leaning forward. "I just wish we could go back to the way things were."

Maria was silent, staring down at her notes.

Ken wiped his palms on his jeans. His left leg was bouncing nervously under the table. *She just needs to figure out how to tell me she feels the same way,* he decided.

"What's the point of all this?" she asked, finally looking up at him from her papers.

Ken recoiled, shocked at the coldness in her tone. But then he reminded himself that Maria was always tough. She obviously wanted an official we-should-get-back-together declaration from him before she said anything.

He took a deep breath. "I know you still care, Maria. So, bottom line? I think we should get back together."

Don't miss any of the books in SWEET VALLEY HIGH SENIOR YEAR, an exciting series from Bantam Books!

#1 CAN'T STAY AWAY
#2 SAY IT TO MY FACE
#3 SO COOL
#4 I'VE GOT A SECRET
#5 IF YOU ONLY KNEW
#6 YOUR BASIC NIGHTMARE
#7 BOY MEETS GIRL
#8 MARIA WHO?
#9 THE ONE THAT GOT AWAY
#10 BROKEN ANGEL
#11 TAKE ME ON
#12 BAD GIRL
#13 ALL ABOUT LOVE
#14 SPLIT DECISION
#15 ON MY OWN
#16 THREE GIRLS AND A GUY
#17 BACKSTABBER
#18 AS IF I CARE
#19 IT'S MY LIFE
#20 NOTHING IS FOREVER
#21 THE IT GUY
#22 SO NOT ME
#23 FALLING APART
#24 NEVER LET GO
#25 STRAIGHT UP
#26 TOO LATE
#27 PLAYING DIRTY
#28 MEANT TO BE
#29 WHERE WE BELONG

Visit the Official Sweet Valley Web Site on the Internet at:

www.sweetvalley.com

Francine Pascal's SVH senioryear

Where We Belong

CREATED BY
FRANCINE PASCAL

BANTAM BOOKS
NEW YORK • TORONTO • LONDON • SYDNEY • AUCKLAND

RL: 6, AGES 012 AND UP

WHERE WE BELONG

A Bantam Book / May 2001

Conceived by Francine Pascal.

Cover photography by Michael Segal.

Produced by 17th Street Productions,
an Alloy Online, Inc. company.
33 West 17th Street
New York, NY 10011.

ISBN: 0-553-49345-0

Visit us on the Web! www.randomhouse.com/teens

Published simultaneously in the United States and Canada

Bantam Books is an imprint of Random House Children's Books, a division of Random House, Inc. BANTAM BOOKS and the rooster colophon are registered trademarks of Random House, Inc. Bantam Books, 1540 Broadway, New York, New York 10036.

PRINTED IN THE UNITED STATES OF AMERICA

OPM 0 9 8 7 6 5 4 3 2 1

To Molly Jessica W. Wenk

Ken Matthews

I'm sick of waiting around for Maria to come to me. I guess if I want us to get back together, I've got to go to her. She'll probably be so relieved to hear me say what's been on her mind all along that we'll be right back to where we were before we broke up.

I hope.

Maria Slater

What's wrong with me? Why can't I get Ken out of my head? After everything he did, I shouldn't even be considering going back to him. If Ken even wants to get back together. What if he doesn't? What if he does?

I don't even know what I'm hoping for anymore.

Conner McDermott

Busted.

Elizabeth Wakefield

Um . . . who is that girl?

CHAPTER 1
A Giant Blank

Conner McDermott only caught a quick glimpse of Alanna's face before she turned and rushed out his kitchen door. But he had seen enough. This was bad. Really bad.

Conner stared after Alanna for a second, dazed. Then he snapped back to Elizabeth, standing there in front of him—inches away, after breaking apart from the intense kiss they'd been in the middle of before Alanna walked into the room.

Elizabeth's blue-green eyes were wide with surprise and confusion, and her mouth hung slightly open.

"Conner—" she started.

Conner blinked. Alanna outside. Elizabeth inside. Elizabeth didn't know about Alanna. Alanna thought he and Elizabeth were over.

"Sorry, I've gotta go," he blurted out before Elizabeth could say another word. He turned and stumbled for the door, letting it slam behind him.

The cool night air felt good on his flushed skin. *Why did Alanna have to pick tonight to show up at my door?* he wondered. *Why that exact moment?*

He caught sight of Alanna fumbling with her car keys across the street and sprinted across the lawn. As he got closer, he realized that her hands were trembling. He winced when he saw the expression on her face—a sickening combination of pain and anger.

Conner knew that look all too well from their days in rehab together. Only this time it was his fault—not her parents' fault or the alcohol's. All he wanted was to grab her and hold her, like he'd done there. But instead he had to explain what she'd just seen—make her understand somehow. He just wished he didn't have to do it tonight, with Elizabeth standing in his kitchen, wondering what was going on.

"Alanna," he said as he came up beside her. "Wait."

She hadn't managed to get the right key in the door anyway, but she kept trying for another couple of seconds, ignoring him. Then she stopped and looked up to meet his gaze.

"At least now I know why you haven't returned any of my calls," she said, her voice hard. Tough. But he knew her better than that. He knew it was all show, just like with him.

Conner stepped closer, his arm nearly brushing hers. He caught his breath, taken off guard by the energy that was still there between them. His eyes dropped down to her soft, full lips, and he imagined kissing her, remembered what it used to feel like. . . .

Alanna jerked back from him, her gray eyes shooting an icy glare, and it hit him why they were out here. He couldn't kiss Alanna—he'd just been kissing Elizabeth. What was the matter with him?

He swallowed, trying to think. "Listen, I'm sorry for being such a jerk," he began. He'd gotten way too used to those words recently. "I mean, about not calling you back. I just didn't know what was going to happen after rehab. How things would . . . work." He sounded so lame. He almost flinched at the sound of his own voice.

She's definitely not going to be satisfied with that, he thought. One thing he'd learned about Alanna was that she had an incredible talent for cutting through excuses and getting right to the truth. He admired it. But right now, he wouldn't have minded if she were a little less sharp.

"Well, it looks like things are *working* out just fine for you," Alanna snapped. "You had your fling with me, and now you're back to your steady girlfriend." She paused, her eyes narrowing. "And she doesn't seem to know anything about me," she continued. "Right?"

Without waiting for an answer, Alanna jammed her key in the lock and swung open the car door.

"No, stop," Conner said, feeling like a helpless idiot. He grabbed her arm as she started to get into the driver's seat, looking her right in the eye and hoping she'd see everything he couldn't get out of his mouth.

She had to know she meant more to him than that. She wasn't just a fling. They had really connected, and he did care about her. That was the problem. If she didn't mean anything, he wouldn't have run after her and be freezing his butt off outside in the dark, especially when there was a warm set of lips waiting for him inside. He shook his head, trying to get the image of Elizabeth out of his mind.

"It's not like that," he said. He dropped his hand from her arm, but she didn't move. "Yes, Elizabeth and I were going out before rehab. But we broke up before I went away. We weren't together when you and I—when I was there." He paused, letting out a short breath. "We're not together now either."

Alanna laughed. "You could have fooled me," she said.

Conner winced and shoved his hands into his jeans pockets. He knew he deserved that, but he wasn't sure what to say. Yeah, he'd kissed Elizabeth. He hadn't known how *not* to. But it didn't mean what Alanna thought.

"Look, Elizabeth is not my girlfriend, okay?" he said. "Not anymore. But it's not like we made any kind of big promises anyway, right? That was the whole thing—living in the now and all that crap."

Alanna nodded. "So I'm right, then," she said. "I was just a distraction. Well, I don't want to keep you any longer, so I'll just—"

"Would you stop?" he blurted out. He shook his head, feeling like it weighed a hundred pounds. He hated this kind of drama. It was exactly the way things *hadn't* been between them at rehab. But here he was, back at home, back in the middle of a bunch of people who needed stuff from him that he couldn't seem to give. "You weren't a distraction, okay?" he said, irritated.

He crossed his arms across his chest, rocking back on his heels. It was getting colder, the wind whipping around him. He didn't want to be out here anymore, having this conversation. And he dreaded the one that waited for him inside his house. Elizabeth would have a million questions for him by the time he got back in there. Why did everything have to be so complicated?

"Conner," Alanna said, her tone softer than it had been all night. "I'm just going to ask you one thing, and then I'm going to leave."

Conner kicked at the ground, wishing he didn't know what was coming.

"Are you and Liz getting back together?" she asked.

Conner's whole body tensed up, hearing the question out loud. He didn't know what he wanted. No, he wanted Elizabeth. But he also wanted Alanna. What he didn't want was to think about any of it.

He sighed, glancing back at Alanna, who stood between the open car door and the front seat, poised to leave.

"I don't know," he answered, not quite meeting her gaze.

"Right," she said, her voice small. Since when did Alanna have such a *small* voice?

This time Conner didn't stop her as she got in her car and shut the door, then turned on the engine and pulled off down the street. He watched until the back lights of her blue Saab disappeared around the corner.

With another deep sigh Conner turned to head back to his house. To the group of friends having his "welcome-home" party without him. To Elizabeth.

Welcome home, Conner, he thought as he trudged up the wet grass to his back door.

Will Simmons cruised down his street, humming along with the radio. He actually felt as good as he had in a long time. At first when he'd gotten to

House of Java and realized that Ken had set him and Melissa up, he'd been furious. But things had turned out okay, and hanging out with Melissa really did make him feel a little like his old self. And there was something he wasn't used to experiencing anymore.

Will smiled as he swung into his driveway. Today had sort of felt like old times—before the tackle that changed everything in a split second. Still, even though he knew Melissa wanted to get back together, he wasn't ready to just dive back in yet. He was going to let her sweat it out a little, pay for the way she'd turned her back on him for Ken Matthews. Then, when he was ready, he'd take her back, and things would be like normal.

Well, in one small way at least.

Will turned off the Blazer's engine and opened the door, maneuvering his crutches out first. At least he was finally able to drive himself around. It wasn't easy with one leg in a cast, but it was better than having his mom take him everywhere.

He hopped out on his good leg, then balanced himself on the crutches as he shut the door. He headed up to the front door, not even minding how long it took him to cross a distance he'd once moved in seconds. He was in a decent mood for the first time he could remember, and he wasn't about to let go of it. He had some tough calculus homework to tackle upstairs, but overall, it was going to be a good night.

"I'm home," he called out once he was inside. His parents were still worried about him getting around by himself, and they usually swarmed on him as soon as he made it through the door.

"In here, honey," his mom shouted back. He followed the sound of her voice into the living room, stopping in the doorway. He frowned, leaning onto the crutches.

"What's going on?" he asked. His parents, who were constantly doing a million things at once, were just sitting there on the couch—the edge of the couch, actually. The television was off, and there was no sign of any newspapers or open books near them. They had been talking. And that usually meant they had been talking about him.

"Will, why don't you sit down?" his father asked, pushing his glasses up his nose.

"Okay," Will said. He sank down onto the plush chair across from the couch, laying his crutches at his feet. He had a sinking feeling that his once happy night was about to be a distant memory.

"We need to have a talk about your future, son," his father said, leaning forward and looking him in the eye. "Your mother and I just aren't sure if you're giving it enough thought." Will's stomach immediately tightened. Just the word *future* made him feel like he was going to puke. He was enjoying the present—as in tonight. Wasn't that enough? Why did his parents always have to bring up the future?

"Will," his mother started. "We know it's been hard for you with the accident and having to come to terms with your football career being over, but have you thought at all about college? A possible career? Honey, we just want what's best for you."

What's best for me is if you leave me alone right now, Will thought. But he didn't say anything. He just sat there staring at them while his mind raced. He couldn't believe they were asking him all of this right now. As if he was supposed to have all the answers to these things that were, like, years away from happening. He had just recently lost the only future he'd ever imagined for himself—as a football star.

He let his gaze wander around the familiar living room. When his parents were seventeen, did they know that they'd have a three-bedroom colonial with a green couch, a front door that squeaked, and a slacker son? Probably not. So what was he supposed to be, some kind of psychic?

"What do you want from me?" he blurted out. His parents looked back at him with equally stunned expressions. "How come I'm supposed to have all the answers?" he demanded, ignoring their reactions.

"Isn't that why it's called the future? Because it's unknown?" He stood up so fast, he almost fell. He grabbed the back of the chair for balance and reached for his crutches.

"Will, we're just saying you should give it some thought," Mrs. Simmons said. "After all, it's—"

"I have thought about it," he interrupted. "It's all I've thought about since the accident. But I still don't know what I'm going to do. So this little talk probably isn't going to help."

Mr. Simmons frowned, deep creases appearing in his forehead. "Listen, young man, we want to talk to you because we're concerned. No, you aren't supposed to have all the answers. But a plan would be good. So sit down."

Will let his crutches fall to the floor and sat back down. He had to hear them out, or they wouldn't let this drop. If he just listened and pretended to care, then maybe he could get out of here fairly soon and make it up to his bedroom. He had never wanted to get to his calc homework so badly.

"It's getting toward the end of your fall semester, Will," his mother said, casting a quick, nervous glance over at his dad.

"It's decision time," Mr. Simmons took over. "You need to figure out just what you're doing before graduation. And you have to do it soon, before the year is over and your friends have left you behind."

Will slouched a little lower in the chair, a kink beginning to form in his lower back from the awkward, stiff position. He already felt left behind. Football had been his future, and now he had nothing. Had his parents forgotten about that?

"I had a plan," he said, clearing the lump that had formed in his throat. "Remember? It's not my fault that it fell through."

Mrs. Simmons's face softened, her eyes filling with sympathy. Pity—there was something he was getting to know really well.

"We know that," she said. "And we're sorry. We know what football meant to you—"

"But your mother and I just want you to know that it's time to think about a different future," Mr. Simmons cut in, his tone more firm than hers. "We made an appointment with Mr. Nelson, the guidance counselor at Sweet Valley, for tomorrow afternoon. There are so many possibilities that we want to make you aware of. Football was only one." He stood, signaling the end of the talk. "The appointment is at four-thirty. We'll meet you at the school. Now, go on, I'm sure you have homework waiting."

Will felt like the wind had been knocked out of him, just like he used to feel after a rough tackle. Football was just one of many possibilities? Were they nuts? Right now he had no future, and the sooner his parents realized it, the better. His future was a giant blank.

Elizabeth was starting to worry she was going to wear a hole in the linoleum floor of Conner's kitchen. Still, she couldn't stop pacing. Because if she stood still, she'd have to let the thoughts in. She'd have to realize what it meant that some girl went flying away after seeing her kiss Conner. She'd have to know that he'd gone after that girl instead of staying to explain to Elizabeth. And worst of all—she'd have to face the fact that that meant this girl, whoever she was, meant something to Conner. Maybe even something more than she did.

Elizabeth shook her head, then glanced up at the clock on the wall above the sink. Had it really only been a few minutes? It seemed like she'd been in here alone for hours.

Maybe I should just leave, she thought, biting her lip. Take off without even waiting for an explanation.

But she didn't want to give Conner an easy out. He owed her . . . something.

She listened to her friends out in the living room, laughing, talking. They had no idea what had just happened in this room. She felt like she was watching a movie—a bad TV movie about someone else's heartbreak.

There's only one reason why a girl would get that upset after watching two people kiss. The pacing wasn't working because she could still hear the words in her head. Elizabeth couldn't believe Conner had already found someone else when they had just broken up. Yeah, she and Evan had almost gotten together while Conner was away, but that was different. They'd been friends already. Elizabeth had never seen that girl before in her life.

At least the pacing was keeping her from staring out the window. Where was he? What if he'd left with her? What if—

Just then the door opened. Elizabeth stopped, looking over in his direction. Her breath caught in her throat when she saw his face.

She wouldn't have thought it was possible to feel both anger and pity at once like this, but it was all there. Conner looked so tired, like he'd just come back from something that had drained him in every imaginable way. She couldn't help feeling that old twinge, seeing him so obviously upset—that old need to reach out and help him. But at the same time she felt an equally strong sense of betrayal and hurt, knowing that for him to be this messed up, he had to really care about that other girl. And how dare he kiss her, in this very room, without telling her there was someone else?

Elizabeth cleared her throat, but he didn't speak. Calmly she walked over to the kitchen table and sat down, intent on making it clear that she wasn't letting him off the hook. She'd come a long way while he was gone. She wasn't just going to melt into a blob of useless need and emotion because he was there.

But then Conner turned his gaze toward her, and as his bright green eyes skimmed her face, her whole body seemed to tremble. This was Conner. Who was she fooling?

Conner coughed. "Look, I'm sorry about that," he said. He ran a hand through his hair. "It's kind of a long story."

Elizabeth pressed her lips together, forcing herself to stay in control. At least she was sitting, so her legs wouldn't give way beneath her.

Conner walked over and sat down at the table across from her. He slumped a little in his chair, and Elizabeth was sure that his leg was pumping up and down underneath the table, just like it always did when he was anxious.

"I, uh, I don't really want to get into it now, if that's okay," he finally said.

Elizabeth glanced down at her hands. Should she

demand an answer? Say she wouldn't leave until he told her what just happened? She looked back up at Conner, hoping he wouldn't make her do it, that he'd be the un-Conner for once and spill everything without being pushed.

Under the harsh light of the overhead kitchen lamp, she noticed the dark rings under his eyes. He didn't just look depressed—he looked defeated.

He's been through so much, she couldn't help thinking. *I can't pump him for information right now.* Yeah, something really big just happened—and she had no idea what any of it meant. But she couldn't press him. Not now.

She sat on her hands, unsure what to do next. Conner seemed to be in another world, and Elizabeth could hear the sounds of the party again, filtering into her crowded brain. She heard Evan's low-pitched, gravelly laugh and then Maria singing along to the song on the radio.

She had to get out of here. She had to, before she demanded to know what was going on from Conner and just ended up making everything worse.

"So, I'm going to go, then," she said, standing. "I'm sure you'll tell me what just happened some other time," she added, trying to sound as casual as possible. Instead her words came out strained and almost cheerful in some strange, twisted way.

But Conner didn't seem to notice. He got up, stretching his arms. "Uh, okay," he said, avoiding her gaze. "I'm pretty beat anyway."

Elizabeth nodded, wondering if he even remembered that not long ago, they'd been standing here wrapped in each other's arms, lost in a kiss that seemed to erase the entire world around them. She could barely remember it herself right now.

Conner moved toward her, and she felt his arm near her side. But he kept going past her and shoved open the swinging door that led through the dining room and into the living room, where everyone was still hanging out.

Elizabeth reached down to straighten her perfectly straight shirt, then followed him out.

Everyone looked up when they entered the room. Out of the corner of her eye Elizabeth saw Maria elbow Tia, and she knew the two of them were sure that she and Conner had gotten back together.

They couldn't be more wrong. A few hours ago she'd actually thought she and Conner had a chance. Now they were further apart than ever.

Elizabeth just hoped no one would ask her what had happened in the kitchen. Right now all she wanted was to get out of there, go home, and crawl under the covers. She scanned the room for Jessica but didn't see her twin.

"Where's Jess?" she asked Maria.

"She took off. She just assumed you'd be here awhile," Maria said, giving Elizabeth a little wink.

Elizabeth held back a groan. On top of everything that had just happened, she now had no ride home. *Great,* she thought.

"So, it's getting pretty late," Evan said. He got up from the arm of the sofa he'd been sitting on. "We'll get outta here and let you settle in, man."

"Thanks," Conner responded. "Thanks, everyone. But yeah, I'm pretty tired." He moved toward the door.

"Hey, Evan," Elizabeth said, walking over to him. "Would you, um, mind driving me home?" She knew he wasn't the best person to be with right now. After all, they had kissed while Conner was in rehab. But he was her friend, and she needed a friend.

Jade, who'd been on the other side of the sofa, stepped closer to Evan, linking her arm through his. "I don't know if we're going straight home," she said before he could respond.

Elizabeth's eyebrows raised slightly. Since when did Evan allow a girlfriend to be his mouthpiece? That wasn't like him at all, and he and Jade had barely been together for, like, two minutes too.

"Actually, I do have to get home," Evan said, flashing Jade a quick smile. He turned back to

Elizabeth. "So yeah, I can drop you off after I take Jade home."

Jade's eyes narrowed, and Elizabeth wondered what the girl's problem was. Right now, though, she didn't really care either way.

This party was officially over.

Will Simmons

What I Want to Do with My Life

~~Play football~~

Be with Melissa??

???????

I know Melissa wants to get back together. It's obvious. I've known her for too long, and I can see right through her. I also know she left me when I was as low as I've ever been. But still, I did my best to push her away.

Maybe I should just go with it. I mean, it's not like anything else in my future is close to certain. At least if I have Melissa, I have something. Something that matters.

Melissa Fox

After tonight I know that Will and I will get back together. There's nothing left of his past—except me. And I know he has way too many good memories to give everything up. I remind him of what his life was like. All I need to do is remind him of what a great girlfriend I can be too. We belong together, and it won't take long for him to see it. He always does.

CHAPTER 2
The Relationship Thing

Elizabeth couldn't help noticing how still the night air seemed as she walked out of Conner's house. It felt the way it did right before—or after—a storm. She shivered, pulling her thin jacket tighter around her.

Without even paying attention to anything else around her, she moved toward Evan's car, walking up next to the passenger side on automatic pilot. Jade arrived next to her and reached out for the handle at the same time she did. Elizabeth pulled back her hand, but Jade did too, staring at her as if this were some kind of test. Who got the front seat? Who got to be the one to back down?

"Hey, guys, get in," Evan called out as he hopped into the driver's seat. Elizabeth decided just to go for it. She didn't feel like standing here all night in this bizarre little war with Jade, especially since she wasn't really clear about what was at stake. She climbed into the front, and Jade got in the back, making a soft huffing sound as she did so and slamming the door a little too hard.

After the night I just had, Jade can deal with riding in the back, Elizabeth thought. Yeah, Jade was dating Evan—and she wasn't—but what was the big deal anyway?

Evan started the ignition and pulled away from Conner's house. Relief washed over Elizabeth. As he drove down the street, her hands slowly released from the tight fists they'd curled into.

"So . . . ," Evan began, giving her a quick glance. He wanted to ask without asking.

Elizabeth opened her mouth to say something, then hesitated. Her first instinct was to pour everything out to Evan, the way she used to. But did she really want him to know about that girl when she didn't even know what the deal was?

He'll find out anyway, she told herself. And she needed someone to listen right now.

"So, everything okay between you and Conner?" Evan asked before she even managed to get a word out, seeming to read her mind.

"Actually, I don't know," Elizabeth admitted, watching the houses pass by out the window. "I think Conner might have a new girlfriend or an old one that just showed up again."

"Really?" Evan said. His grip on the steering wheel tightened, and he checked his side-view mirror, avoiding her eyes.

Does he know something? she wondered. It hadn't even occurred to her that Conner would have told his other friends about that girl.

"See, we were in the kitchen—" she began.

"Yeah, for a while," Evan said, smiling.

Elizabeth shook her head. "Well, *I* was in there for a while, but Conner was only there for a few minutes," she said. "And we . . . things were going pretty well." She stopped, letting herself recall the way it had felt to have his lips on hers again after all this time. She sighed. "But then this girl just walked right in, through the back door. She saw us kissing and then ran back out. She was really upset. Conner ran after her and left me in the kitchen for what seemed like forever. When he came back inside, he said he didn't want to talk about it all. He looked so tired, I just let it go. But I didn't want to. I wanted to know who that was."

"Mm-hmm." Evan nodded, staring straight ahead. "You did the right thing, though. Conner's still pretty stressed out."

"I know," Elizabeth said, looking out the window, watching the mailboxes zoom by. "But it's just going to drive me crazy not knowing who she was or why she freaked out like that. If he hadn't just gotten home from rehab, I might have pushed him to tell me who she was and why he went after her. But I really want him to get better. I know that's more important than me, or us, or whatever." She stared down at her fingers, picking at the old polish.

"That's true," Evan said, "but remember, we're his friends no matter what. If we don't stick our noses into his personal life, who will?" he joked, giving her a little nudge.

Elizabeth couldn't help but crack a smile. Evan always knew exactly what to say. Shouldn't she know that by now?

"Yeah, maybe you're right," she agreed. "But he should want to tell me unless he's hiding something." She felt tears start to collect in her eyes, and it hit her just how hurt she really was right now. "I guess—maybe I did think we'd get back together all this time I was saying I wasn't sure," she said. "And you know, I think he kind of thought so too. And then this girl . . ."

Elizabeth heard a throat clear and winced. She had completely forgotten that Jade was even in the car. Evan obviously had too because he quickly checked the rearview mirror and turned back toward her. "Everything okay back there, Jade?"

"Yeah, I'm all right," Jade said quietly.

Elizabeth wondered if that was really true. Jade was a friend of Jessica's, and they'd always gotten along okay. But tonight Jade was acting pretty strange with her. Jade had to know that Elizabeth and Evan had sort of had a thing, and now she was sitting here listening to someone she barely knew go on and on about her messed-up relationship. Elizabeth felt a pang of guilt for taking the front seat.

Evan pulled up in front of Jade's apartment complex. "Door-to-door service," he announced, unbuckling his seat belt.

"Thanks," Jade said. "See you." She quickly got out of the car and started striding across the lawn, ignoring the fact that Evan had been halfway out of his seat, ready to walk her to her front door.

"Guess she was in a rush," he said. He shrugged as he slid back inside and rebuckled his belt. Still, he watched from there until Jade had made it inside the courtyard and safely into her apartment.

"I, um, I think maybe she was a little annoyed about me coming along," Elizabeth volunteered. "Maybe you should give her a call when you get home."

Elizabeth felt another one of those guilty pangs. She hadn't meant to ruin Evan and Jade's night. But wasn't what she'd just been through enough to justify her being selfish for once?

"So, what next?" Evan asked as he headed toward her house.

"I thought you'd tell me," she only half joked. She

really wasn't sure what to do next. Should she wait for Conner to come to her? Demand to know who the girl was tomorrow in the hallway at school?

"I still think you and Conner will get back together someday," he said. "He just got back from rehab, after all. I think he's made some major strides. Soon he might be ready for another try at the relationship thing."

Elizabeth slumped down in her seat, aware that Evan had actually been trying to cheer her up. She knew he was probably right too. It was pretty early for Conner to jump back into a relationship. But her fear was that when he was ready for another relationship, it wouldn't be with her.

Ken Matthews turned up the cheesy love song playing on the radio. He was in a great mood, and nothing could get in the way of it. When Tia had told him that Maria still had feelings for him, he'd known exactly what he had to do. Of course, he still hadn't gone through with it all day in school, but now he was determined. He and Maria had wasted enough time.

Maria's house had never seemed so far away. Ken eased up on the accelerator, realizing he'd been going pretty fast. He glanced in the rearview mirror, checking for local cops. He didn't want to get pulled over before he made it to the Slater house.

"I love you, baby." He was even singing along, his fingers serving as drumsticks on the steering wheel. It had been too long since he had driven to Maria's.

The song came to an end, and the DJ's voice boomed out through the speakers, babbling about what a beautiful Wednesday night it was here in California.

Suddenly Ken pulled his Trooper over to the side of the road as what the guy said sank in. It was Wednesday night! And it hadn't been long enough for him to forget that Wednesday night was usually Maria's study-at-House-of-Java night. She hadn't been there earlier, but she was probably there now since her family's dinner should be done by this point. Luckily House of Java was even closer than the Slater house. He was more than ready to get this whole conversation out of the way and just start over.

Ken pulled away from the curb and made a left at the first light toward the coffeehouse. He could almost smell Maria's perfume. He already imagined the way his shirt was going to smell just like her when he left HOJ tonight. If he got lucky, he might also be tasting some of her cherry lip gloss. But the most important thing was that they were going to be back together—where they belonged.

Ken pulled the Trooper into a spot near the door

of House of Java and hopped out, humming the tune that had been playing on the radio. He walked up to the coffeehouse entrance, feeling lighter and more carefree than he had in weeks.

He pulled open the door and was instantly greeted with the warm, wafting smell of coffee. Ken didn't even have to look around the nearly empty store to find Maria. There was a couple snuggling over mugs in the corner and an old man reading a paper near the counter. But Maria always tried to get the same booth, the quiet one in the back near the rest rooms. She liked to down a few mochaccinos, and being near the rest room was important to her. So was the fact that she could actually get some studying done there.

Ken let his eyes wander to where he expected to find her . . . and sure enough, there she was. Her notes and books were spread out all around her, and two empty mugs were on the table. He took in her dark, smooth skin and the graceful curve of her neck.

This has to work, he thought, his heart rate speeding up. *We've been apart for way too long.*

"Hi!" he said brightly, striding toward her.

Maria glanced up, her eyes widening in surprise. "Ken," she said. She looked behind him, as if checking to see who was there with him.

She thinks I have a date or something, Ken thought.

"I'm here alone," he said quickly. "Actually—I came to talk to you."

Maria held his gaze for a moment, her expression impossible to read. But he was almost positive he saw a glint of a smile in her eyes—just for a second.

"Well, sit down," she said, pushing her papers aside. "Sorry for the mess. I am so swamped right now with this scene for drama class."

Ken sank down into the chair across from her, then linked his hands on the table. He let out a nervous laugh, and Maria cocked her head to the side, obviously waiting for him to say why he was here.

Ken cleared his throat. There was no point in putting this off another minute.

"Look. I just wanted you to know that Melissa and I are over," he blurted out.

Maria's eyebrows shot up. She twirled a pencil around in her fingers, pressing her lips together. "Why are you telling *me* this?" she asked.

Ken blinked. Why wouldn't he tell her? Who else even mattered?

"Because, Maria, I did some crazy, stupid stuff," he explained. "And I want you to know it's all done now. I never really wanted to be with Melissa anyway. I only felt sorry for her after everything that happened with Will." He paused, leaning forward. "I just wish we could go back to the way things were."

Maria was silent, staring down at her notes.

Ken wiped his palms on his jeans. His left leg was bouncing nervously under the table. *She just needs to figure out how to tell me she feels the same way,* he decided.

"What's the point of all this?" she asked, finally looking up at him from her papers.

Ken recoiled, shocked at the coldness in her tone. But then he reminded himself that Maria was always tough. She obviously wanted an official we-should-get-back-together declaration from him before she said anything. Luckily Ken was ready to play along. Whatever it took to get her back.

He took a deep breath. "I know you still care, Maria. So, bottom line? I think we should get back together."

A huge smile spread across his face as he waited for her to light up, to throw herself into his arms and admit she'd just been too stubborn to say the same thing.

But again there was silence. Then Maria jumped to her feet and began stacking her papers and books. Calmly she opened her backpack and started putting things away.

"Uh, Maria?" Ken scratched his head, his smile fading. "Aren't you going to answer?"

"What am I supposed to say to that, Ken?" she asked, still keeping herself busy with her stuff and avoiding his gaze. "Honestly, I couldn't care less about you after everything you've pulled. And I can't believe you think you can just walk in here and try to take back everything that's happened. Did you expect me to fall into your arms and cry with gratitude or something?"

Ken gaped at her, feeling ill. His whole body was frozen, and he couldn't think of a single thing to say in response. Why had Tia told him Maria wanted him back if she didn't?

Maria finished putting everything in her bag and swung it over her shoulder. "I'll see you later," she mumbled, then rushed out of HOJ.

Ken's leg began pumping under the table again, nearly banging his knee against the hard surface. He couldn't believe he had poured out his heart like a jerk and she'd left him with just a few sharp words. He stared at one of her empty glass coffee mugs, trying to make sense of what he'd just experienced. Only a few minutes ago he'd been on top of the world, and now he felt like crawling under this table and never coming out.

Maria felt like she could barely breathe as she stepped outside, closing the door on HOJ and Ken.

Where did that come from? He knew *she* still cared? She felt like screaming. How dare he walk in there and act like he was doing the supreme good thing by letting her know Melissa was out and she was back in? Where was the apology for how much he'd hurt her? She almost wanted to go back in and yell at him some more, really let him have it.

But if she did—if she allowed herself to face him again—then she might have to admit how strong the urge was to do exactly what he must have expected her to do. One look into his sweet, caring blue eyes and she would have been a total goner.

So instead she'd go somewhere else. Talk to someone who'd put some sense back into her.

Like Elizabeth, Maria decided as she climbed into her car and took off down the street. Elizabeth was the one person who could understand the complete and utter frustration Maria felt with Ken, because Elizabeth was going through it with Conner.

Maria rolled down the window of her mother's Volvo and felt the night air hit her face. It was just what she needed. That, and a three-hour gripe session with Elizabeth over guys and what they could possibly be thinking. She switched on the radio, and immediately a sad love song came on midchorus. It was a new release from the current it band that seemed to be on constantly everywhere she went.

Right now was not the time for it, though. She changed the station to one of her mom's presets, a nice calming, classical station.

As she pulled into the Wakefield driveway, Maria noticed the Jeep was gone. She hoped that Jessica had gotten away with the car tonight and not Elizabeth. That one little thing might be just what she needed to send her over the edge. And she really didn't want to cry over Ken. She'd promised herself she wouldn't give the guy one more tear.

With a deep breath, Maria got out and walked up to the Wakefields' front door. It was getting late for a school night, and she hoped Elizabeth's parents wouldn't mind her stopping by. She could always say it was for a study session, which was the excuse she'd give her own parents. She knocked on the heavy oak door and waited, listening to the sound of approaching footsteps in the hall before the door swung open.

"Hi, Maria!" Mrs. Wakefield said brightly, the television remote control in her hand.

"Sorry to stop by so late," Maria apologized.

Mrs. Wakefield shook her head. "It's always nice to have you here," she said. "Come on in. Liz is upstairs."

Relief washed over Maria as she took the stairs two at a time. She knocked softly on Elizabeth's door. She could hear the strains of a slow song coming from inside. As she listened, she realized it was the same song she'd heard earlier in her car.

Someone else has love-life problems. At least I'm not alone here.

"Liz?" she called, opening the door a crack and peering in. Elizabeth was lying on her bed on her stomach, her face propped on a striped pillowcase. She was already in her pajamas and looked like she'd completed phase one of the get-ready-for-bed thing. Normally Maria would feel guilty for stopping by so late, but she needed her best friend more than ever.

"Hey, Maria," Elizabeth said, finally noticing her standing in the doorway. "How long have you been there? I think I was zoning."

"Just a second," Maria answered, walking in. She was already taking off her jacket and pulling up a chair. "Sorry for coming over so late without calling first. But I just saw Ken, and I had to talk to you about it. I have no idea what's going on or what I should do."

Elizabeth groaned. "I can relate to that. There must be something in the air. Is there a full moon or something?"

They both laughed, but Maria noticed the red around her friend's eyes. Elizabeth had been crying—maybe her story was harsher than Maria's.

"Hey, do you want to go first?" Maria joked. "Something with Conner, I'm guessing?"

Elizabeth winced. "God, I can't even hear the stupid guy's name," she moaned. "No, tell me about Ken first. I could use the distraction."

"Well, it's probably more simple than it seems," Maria said, stretching out her long legs. "I just lied through my teeth to Ken."

"What?" Elizabeth sat up and settled into a cross-legged position at the end of her bed. "What happened?"

Maria sighed. "I was at House of Java studying, and Ken waltzes in and starts saying how he knows I want to get back together and how he thinks we should too. He said things were over with Melissa, and he even admitted he was stupid to go out with her." Maria allowed a small smile to creep over her face. "I could have told him that," she muttered. "But anyway," she continued, raising her voice again, "I ended up walking out on him and telling him I didn't care, which, by the way, I wish were true."

Elizabeth let out a deep breath and shook her head. "Wow," she said. "I'm sorry, Maria. But why didn't you tell him how you felt? I don't get it."

"How can I go back to him after everything that's happened?" Maria asked. "After everything he's done to me? He still doesn't seem to get it, you know? He just thought he could say that, and things would be fine again. But he ditched me for football and Melissa

Fox. Hello? That's major. Can I really forgive that?"

Elizabeth glanced down at her bed, fiddling with the ruffle on her bedspread. "I don't know. What are we supposed to do when a guy chooses someone else over us?"

Maria narrowed her eyes, realizing that Elizabeth wasn't just talking about her and Ken. "Hey, what happened with Conner?" she asked. "You guys were in the kitchen together for a while, so I figured it was all good." She paused. "Although you didn't look like you were in great shape when you left with Evan. I'm sorry—I should have talked to you then."

"No, it's fine," Elizabeth reassured her. "I really just wanted to get out of there. And yeah, things were great with us at first." Her eyes started to gleam with fresh tears. "We even kissed," she admitted. "But then some—some *girl* walked in the room. Maria, I don't know who she was. But when she saw me and Conner together, she freaked and ran out. And Conner went after her. Then when he finally came back inside, he wouldn't tell me who she was or what had just happened."

Maria reached out and gave Elizabeth's hand a sympathetic squeeze. "I'm sorry, Liz," she said. "That's really rough. You know, you're right—there must be a full moon. I mean, what is going on here? What do Conner and Ken want from us?"

"I wish I knew," Elizabeth said. "I also wish I could help you out more, but right now I am in no place to give anyone advice on relationships."

"I'm still glad I came over," Maria said, managing a small smile. "Just knowing there's someone else in pain makes me feel better," she teased.

Elizabeth tossed a pillow at her, and Maria caught it, then threw it back, laughing.

"So, what do you think you're going to do?" Elizabeth asked, her brief smile already disappearing.

Maria shrugged. "I wish there were, like, rules for this," she said. "You know, something that tells you exactly how much you should take and when it's too much to ever forgive them."

"I definitely think cheating should end the relationship," Elizabeth said.

"But what's cheating?" Maria asked. "I mean, if you've already broken up, that's not really cheating, right?"

"I guess not." Elizabeth sighed. "You and Ken had already broken up when he started going out with Melissa. And this girl . . . I mean, Conner and I aren't technically together anymore."

They were quiet, and Maria noticed that the sad love ballad had been replaced by a cheery, upbeat song that was completely out of place in the room.

"I know this sounds pretty lame," Elizabeth

began. She glanced over at her stereo. "Maybe this music is affecting my brain," she added. "The thing is, you know I can't stand clichés, but sometimes they really seem to make sense. Like the one about following your heart?"

Maria nodded. "Yeah, it sounds good on paper. But how are you supposed to follow your heart when it's chasing its own tail?"

Elizabeth laughed. "Cute," she said. "I don't know, but I think I need to get some sleep."

"Yeah, me too," Maria agreed. "Thanks for talking. I'll see you tomorrow." She stood and slipped her jacket back on, then headed for the door.

"'Night," Elizabeth said, already crawling under the covers.

Maria closed the door behind her and let out a deep breath. She knew what her heart was telling her—she was only wondering if she should listen.

Maria Slater

Reasons to Take Ken Back

1. *We were so great together at first, and maybe it could be like that again.*
2. *He has been trying to make it up to me.*
3. *I don't think I can stand seeing him with Melissa Fox again. (That counts for more than one, I think.)*
4. *It's good to be with someone who has different interests. It makes things more exciting.*
5. *I miss him like I've never missed anyone in my life.*

Jade Wu

I'm finally with a guy who really makes me happy and doesn't seem to expect me to be anything else than what I am. Then why do I feel like something bad has to happen? As soon as Elizabeth Wakefield came along for the ride today, I totally flipped for no reason. He's into me now, not her. He even called after he dropped her off and said he was sorry if he seemed rude, but he was just worried about "his friend."

Friend. See, maybe that's the problem. "My friend" is what Jeremy called Jessica by the time he started dating me. And look how that turned out. So excuse me if I'm a tiny bit paranoid. I think I've earned the right to be.

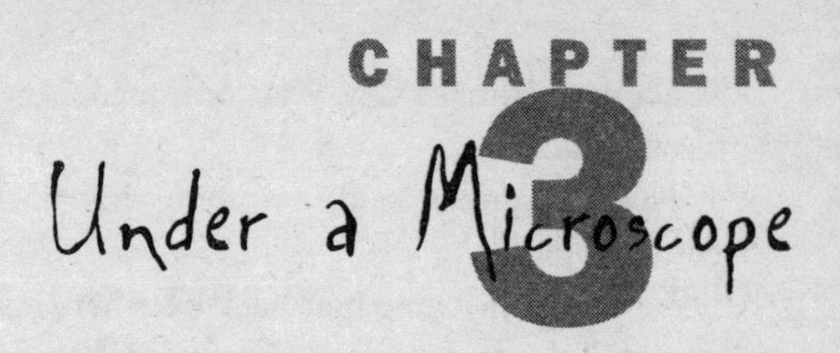

CHAPTER 3
Under a Microscope

A steady, pelting rain hit Conner as he stepped out of his car on Thursday morning. It hardly ever rained in sunny Sweet Valley, but the weather matched Conner's rotten mood.

If I can just get through this day without having to analyze everything, I might be okay, he thought as he headed inside and cut a path to his locker. No such luck. Tia was stationed right in front of his locker, her arms crossed and her face set in a determined stare.

"Hey, Tee," he said. "Is this more of that welcome-back stuff? Because I've been at school all week now. I think I'm officially welcomed."

"Yeah, well, you know. It can be hard to jump right back into everything, right?" she asked. "Especially, um, relationships with . . . people."

Conner tried not to wince. He knew exactly where this was headed.

"I wasn't sure, you know, if maybe you'd want to

talk about anything today," Tia continued. "Anything on your mind?"

"Nope," Conner said, propping his backpack against his locker.

Tia flipped her long hair back over her shoulder. "Hmmm," she said. "A lot's gone on since you were here, and I know a lot happened to you in rehab too. There must be something you want to tell me."

"Listen, Tee. I've got nothing for you," he said.

Tia let out an exasperated sigh. "Conner, I know that something's going on. You and Liz were way too cold to each other after you left the kitchen last night. Just spill, okay?"

"It's fine," Conner replied, spinning the combination on his lock. *Does she have to push me first thing in the morning?* he wondered. Then again, with Tia it didn't matter what time of day it was if there was gossip to be shared.

"I just wanted to remind you that I'm your friend as much as I am Elizabeth's," Tia said. "You can trust me, McDermott."

"Thanks, but there's nothing to tell," Conner said. He grabbed his books for first and second periods, then slammed his locker shut.

He thought the loud bang would finally give Tia a clue, but she didn't move. She just stood there, waiting for him to share his "feelings," like he'd had to do a million times in rehab. Couldn't his friends at least give him a break from the third degree?

I'm doing it again, he thought, frowning. One of the promises he'd made to himself while he was away was not to jump all over people in his life for just trying to show that they cared. And Tia was number one at the top of the list—of both the people who cared *and* the people he'd jumped on.

Plus Tia knew Elizabeth pretty well. Maybe she could even give some actually useful advice here.

Conner shifted his weight from one foot to the other. There was at least ten minutes before the bell, and he wasn't going to get rid of Tia anytime before then without talking.

"I don't mean to push you," Tia jumped in before he could begin. "You can come to me whenever you're ready. I just know that if I were you, I'd want to talk to someone. I mean, after all you've been through . . ."

Conner shook his head, smiling. Maybe those ten minutes could be filled up after all.

". . . the whole Liz thing even without the drinking is something to talk about—"

"Listen, Tee," Conner finally cut her off. "I hooked up with someone else at rehab. Her name is Alanna, and she showed up last night while I was kissing Liz. Happy now? You know what happened."

Tia's dark eyes widened to full Tia capacity. "You met a girl at *rehab?*" she asked. "Isn't that against all their rules and everything?"

Conner leaned up against the wall. "Yeah, sort of," he admitted. "But it wasn't like that. It was just . . . I felt like my whole life was under a microscope the entire time I was there. Alanna got that. We were going through the same stuff, and we understood each other. It was no pressure."

Was. That had sure changed fast.

"Well, what are you going to do about Liz, then?" Tia asked. "I mean, are you and Alanna still together?"

Elizabeth. That was the big question. Everyone wanted an answer—including him.

He and Alanna had so much in common. From everything she'd said about growing up and the way her family was, it was like they'd lived the same life. They fit together more naturally than anything he'd ever experienced. But it wasn't that simple—because he couldn't get Elizabeth out of his mind. It was almost like his thing with Elizabeth was more of an obsession.

Or an addiction. He couldn't help hearing his old counselor, Jeff, in his head, talking about addictive personalities and how easy it can be to transfer an addiction from one thing to another. Wasn't it best to get all addictions out of his system?

"Um, Conner?" Tia prompted.

He refocused on her, noticing that the hall was starting to fill with people and early morning commotion.

"Tee, I honestly don't know what's going to happen," he told her. "But I bet you have something all ready to tell me, right?"

"Nope, nothing," Tia said. "I'm just here to listen."

Wow. Tia the advice giver had nothing to say to him? If he could stump her, then he really did have a tough decision in front of him.

"Uh—okay. Thanks," Conner said.

The warning bell rang through the halls, shrill and piercing. Conner was still getting used to that sound again. There hadn't been any bells in rehab.

I wish there'd been a warning bell before Alanna walked in last night, he thought. Maybe he'd still have to deal with this, but at least he could have stalled a little longer.

"Conner, everything's going to work out," Tia said. "You just got home. Give yourself some slack. Okay?"

"Yeah, sure," Conner said. But he definitely didn't feel very hopeful right now. And talking about it hadn't helped him solve *this* problem. Conner knew it was going to take more than talk to figure out what he was going to do about Alanna and Elizabeth.

* * *

Ken played the scene with Maria at HOJ over and over in his mind as he headed down the SVH hallway. He'd already run it through a million times last night before he went to sleep, but he wasn't getting too far. Why had she gone so crazy on him? What had he said wrong?

He'd hardly been able to drag himself out of bed this morning. The thought of facing her after last night was way too rough. She sure seemed convinced that getting back together was not the right move. But how did she know that? And how was she able to be so *calm* about it all?

Ken stopped, nearly getting trampled by the freshmen guys walking behind him. He moved to the side of the hallway, trying to think. That was just it—the way she acted like she didn't care about what he'd said. He knew that she only used that supercalm act when she was trying to hide her true feelings.

He leaned over and took a drink of water from the fountain, trying to ignore the glob of gum that was stuck in the drain. He wiped his mouth with the back of his sleeve.

Maybe her reaction came from the fact that she *did* still have feelings for him, but she was afraid to let him know it. *Or afraid to face it herself,* he realized.

Man, too bad he wasn't taking a class in psychology. He could probably ace it, he was so good at this! The more he thought about it, the more it made sense. Maybe Maria still cared and it was up to him to figure out how to prove it to her and win her back. That was it, he knew it.

Unfortunately, he had no idea how to make her realize that she was lying to herself and to him.

"Hi, Ken!"

Sara Riley, a cute sophomore cheerleader with bouncy brown curls, walked by with her group of giggling friends.

"Hi," he said quickly. Ever since he'd become star of the football team again, girls like Sara were practically everywhere. It was just too bad that they weren't the girls Ken cared about.

But maybe that's the way to get Maria to open her eyes, he thought. If Maria could see what she was missing, she'd want him back. He'd seen the way she looked at him and Melissa when they were together.

As he walked into history class, Ken scanned the room for the right girl to make Maria jealous. Luckily there was a cute girl sitting right next to his usual seat. He'd barely noticed her all semester, but he was pretty sure he remembered her name was Abby from attendance roll call.

Ken was racking his brain, trying to think of a way to strike up a conversation with her, when Maria walked in and took her seat toward the back of the classroom. Ever since they'd broken up, she'd started sitting back there. He gave her a small smile, but Maria ignored him. She was definitely not over their confrontation last night.

I can't believe she's going to play this game of the injured girlfriend, Ken thought. Maria was usually so straightforward, almost blunt. It was one of the things he loved most about her and definitely one of the things he missed most.

It was time to put his plan into action. Luckily Mr. Ford was late, which gave him an opening. Ken turned to Abby. "Why is it that we have to wait for teachers when they're late, but they can't excuse us for being late?" he asked.

Abby smiled and rolled her eyes, turning her whole body toward Ken. She was definitely ready to flirt. Ken felt a surge of relief mixed with anxiety. Was this the right move? He checked on Maria out of the corner of his eye, but she was digging around in her backpack. Probably looking for a pen that worked. She never seemed to have pens that wrote.

"I know," Abby said, snapping his attention back to her. "Mr. Ford is known for being late. My sister had him four years ago, and he was the same way then too. She's in college now."

"At least in college you can skip class if you don't feel like going," he said.

"I know, I can't wait for college," Abby said, her light eyes beaming. "I'm trying to get in somewhere down south. I'd really like to go to Vanderbilt or Duke. How about you?"

Ken barely heard her question. He was too busy pretending not to watch Maria. He had definitely gotten her attention with this little flirting match. But instead of looking jealous, Maria's gaze was as cold and distant as it had been the night before.

"Good morning, class. Sorry I'm late!" Mr. Ford said as he rushed in the room. "I was up pretty late last night, poring over your tests. But they're finally graded."

Abby stopped talking but smiled at Ken as she faced front.

Ken was relieved that he could finally drop the act. Abby was nice and seemed smart, but he wasn't interested in anyone except Maria.

Maria. She sure didn't seem jealous about what had just happened. It only seemed to make her care even less. He hadn't expected her to fall into his arms right there or anything, but it just seemed like he'd pushed her even further away instead of getting closer.

This is going to be harder than I thought, he realized. *I need to move on to plan B. But first I need a plan B.*

* * *

You need help, Simmons, Will thought. Will had been up half the night, trying to come up with a solution to the big question of what he was going to do with his future. The only conclusion he had come to was that he couldn't do this alone.

He had gotten an idea in first-period study hall and managed to snag a pass. Coach Riley had always given him good advice when he was starting quarterback. Of course, that was the giant, gaping difference between two months ago and now. Could Coach give him the advice he needed to get through this afternoon's meeting with his parents and Mr. Nelson?

Will paused just a moment before adjusting his crutches under his arms and knocking on Coach Riley's door. *Please let him have some good words of advice,* Will hoped. Or at least maybe an escape plan to let Will avoid this stupid after-school meeting altogether.

The door swung open, and Coach Riley stood in front of him. When he saw Will, a brief expression of surprise crossed his sunburned face, quickly replaced by his usual gruff almost-smile.

"Will, hello," he greeted him. "How's it going?"

"Hey, Coach," Will said. "I—I was wondering if I could talk to you for a second?"

"Well, I was just about to step out for a cup of

coffee, but that can wait. Come on in." Coach Riley beckoned Will to step inside his small office. It was hard to navigate with his crutches, but Coach pulled up a chair, and Will sat down.

"What's this all about?" Coach Riley asked, taking his own seat at his desk, which was stacked with piles of papers and manila folders.

Will's gaze traveled around Coach Riley's once all-too-familiar office, observing all the relics of his old life. The glass case next to the coach's desk was jam-packed with division and sectional trophies. Players' red-and-white jerseys lined the walls. This was once his world—but Will needed to move on. That was why he was here.

"How're your classes going?" Coach Riley prompted when Will didn't answer. Will's eyes darted back to his old coach, and he saw that the man was studying Will's face for signs that something might be wrong.

"Uh, they're okay," he answered mechanically. "But what I really need is some advice," he blurted out.

"Shoot," said Coach, looking relieved that they were finally getting to the point.

"What do you think an injured ballplayer should do next?" Will asked, staring at his hands.

"I assume we're talking about you here?" Coach Riley asked.

Will managed a small smile. "Yeah, me," he responded.

"Well, you, my man, have a lot of options," Coach said. He rested his hands behind his head and put his feet up on the desk. "What you need to do is make sure you get a college degree so you don't close off any options," he began. "Now more than ever, your grades are going to help you get ahead in life or make you fall behind."

Will nodded. Coach Riley was sounding way too much like his dad. Will knew he needed to work on getting his grades up. They weren't horrible, but they could be better. Still, grades . . . college . . . what did it all matter if he didn't even know what he wanted to do?

"Sports can still be a part of your life," Coach Riley continued. "There are other ways to be involved in sports than just being a player. Have you ever considered being a coach?"

A coach? Will cringed automatically at the image. "No way," he said without thinking. "I mean, I'm sure it's a great job," he added quickly, realizing he'd just eaten his foot for lunch. "I just don't know if I'd be able to do it."

"I think you'd make a fine coach," Coach Riley said, bringing his feet down off the desk and moving forward in his chair. "When I was all of twenty-two and just out of college, I thought I'd turn pro," he went on. "But it didn't turn out the way I expected. Sure, I was good for a losing division-one school, but I wasn't a star of a winning team. Those are the players they pick for the big leagues. I decided that coaching was the best way for me to stay connected to a game I love."

Will was only half listening to Coach Riley's speech. He was glad that the guy seemed to like what he did, but this wasn't exactly helping Will. He needed a more concrete plan. He also wasn't sure he had it in him to coach others on to glory while his time had passed. He was only seventeen—his career shouldn't be over. It had barely even begun. He sighed, then shoved his hand through his hair. Somehow he felt like there was suddenly less air in the room—like he had to get out of here fast.

"Thanks, Coach. I'll think about it," Will said, rising to his feet and grabbing the crutches he'd propped next to the chair. "I really need to get back to study hall now. This pass isn't good for the entire period."

There weren't any easy answers to this problem. Maybe there weren't even any answers at all.

Coach Riley rose to his feet as well. "Feel free to come back and talk anytime." He offered his hand to Will, and Will shook it firmly.

"Whoa, there!" Coach Riley said with a grin.

"Your leg may be ruined, but there's nothing wrong with your handshake. It's just as strong as ever."

How lame! Will thought. What a stupid thing for Coach Riley to say. If Will were a coach, he'd make sure he said more positive things to his players. *If* he were a coach. Maybe it wasn't such a bad idea. Hey, it was an idea at least. And one that he could probably make a reality. He definitely had the enthusiasm for the game and the skills to coach.

But he was supposed to be a player. He had put everything into football, and now he had nothing to show for it. It was all he had ever cared about, besides Melissa. Now he had neither.

"Liz, I'm glad you're here."

Elizabeth whipped her head around at the sound of the voice. She'd been totally lost in this late article she was trying to wrap up for the next *Oracle* issue. She'd been relieved to have an excuse to hide out in the school newspaper office. It meant avoiding . . . people. And with everything that had been going on lately, she hadn't done much at the paper anyway. She still needed to draft an article on school parking spaces and arrange a staff meeting about the Christmas dance.

But there went the whole alone thing. Megan Sandborn, Conner's little sister of all people, was standing in the doorway of the office. "Can we talk?" she asked.

Elizabeth nodded, and Megan walked inside the room, glancing around to see if anyone else was around.

"It's just me," Elizabeth said.

At least, it was *just me,* she thought. Elizabeth loved hanging out with Megan, but Megan reminded her of Conner—which was the exact thing she wasn't supposed to be thinking about.

"Is everything okay?" she asked Megan.

"Actually, I wanted to ask if everything was okay with *you,*" Megan said. She put her backpack on the floor and hoisted herself up onto one of the desks. "I know about that girl," Megan went on. "Even though Conner sometimes acts like I'm invisible. I just want you to know that I think you and Conner are good for each other and I want you to get back together."

Elizabeth hesitated. She wasn't sure just how much Megan actually knew about what had happened, and she was sure that Conner wouldn't be too happy about her getting into all of this with his sister. He was way protective when it came to her. But Megan did seem to understand what was happening, and it felt good to have someone care.

"Thanks, Megan," Elizabeth said. "That's really nice, but I'm not sure what your brother's going to do."

"Excuse me?"

Elizabeth almost jumped at the deep voice, and she and Megan both turned to see Conner standing where Megan had been just minutes before. His eyes were narrowed defiantly, and he was giving Elizabeth a serious glare.

"What's going on?" he asked, walking over to them. "Liz, Megan shouldn't be involved in what's between you and me," he said, his voice growing louder. "Besides, if you're digging for information, Megan doesn't know anything."

Megan hopped off the desk and faced her brother. "I may not know everything that's going on," she said, "but I do know that there's a problem between you and Liz. I was worried about her, so I came here to talk to her. She didn't ask me any questions or pump me for information. So if you're going to be mad at someone, be mad at me, or better yet, yourself!" She snatched up her backpack and stormed out of the room.

An awkward silence filled the air, and Elizabeth fought the urge to follow Megan out. She was afraid of whatever would come out of Conner's mouth next. Afraid of what would come out of *hers* too.

"Uh, sorry," Conner mumbled in a barely audible voice. "I just figured—I was wrong, I guess." He glanced down at his beat-up boots. When he looked back up, he met Elizabeth's eyes.

"I'm sorry about last night too," he said, shoving his hands in his jeans pockets. "See, this is the problem. I'm always messing up your life, making you upset. I'm tired of it."

Elizabeth tugged on the sleeves of her thin turtleneck sweater. "It hasn't been easy, Conner," she acknowledged. "But I've definitely gotten stronger. And I know you've never hurt me on purpose." She got up and walked over to him, taking his hand in hers. "We can be okay," she said softly, interlacing her fingers with his. The warmth of his skin almost made it hard to speak. "What do you think?" she asked, drawing closer to him.

Conner stared down at her, and she could see in his eyes that he wanted to kiss her as badly as she wanted to kiss him. "I believe you," he said, his voice husky. He started to lean down toward her, and she tilted her head, waiting. But suddenly he stopped, pulling his hand free of hers and backing away from her.

"This isn't right," he said, running a hand over his hair. "Liz, that girl the other night? Her name is Alanna. We—We hooked up in rehab."

Elizabeth felt her eyes fill with tears, but she blinked to keep them back. She didn't want to cry in front of Conner. Even though she and Evan had gotten close too, somehow it hurt more than she could understand that Conner had been with someone else. Still, they'd been broken up. He hadn't done anything wrong, and they could get past it, just like she'd moved on from Evan. But there was one question that had to be answered first.

Elizabeth swallowed. "So, who do you want to be with now, Conner?" she asked. "Me or Alanna?"

As soon as the words came out, she wanted to take them back. But she had to know—because she'd sworn that she wouldn't let Conner take over her life and wreck her again like he had before, and that meant getting the truth and dealing with it, whatever it was.

"Well?" she said.

"I don't know," Conner replied.

Ken Matthews

Plan B

Be honest with yourself, Matthews. There is no plan B. You never even really had a plan A. But I think that little trick to try and get Maria jealous by flirting with some random girl only made her more mad. What can I do to convince her we belong together? I guess I have to keep trying.

To: smilegrl@ipex.net
From: alannaf@swiftnet.com
Subject: A great guy

Hey!

I know I haven't been around in a while, but I have news. I met an amazing guy—he is so gorgeous! Only problem is he has an ex and I guess he's not really over her. But they're totally wrong for each other, so I'm sure he'll choose me. Do you think it's okay that I told him a couple of teeny tiny lies about me? I mean, it's all stuff that's pretty much true, but he probably wouldn't get it if I told him the full story. That's fine, right?

XO

Alanna

To: alannaf@swiftnet.com
From: smilegrl@ipex.net
Subject: re: A great guy

Hey, Alanna!

I figured you were out of the picture because of a guy. How cute is he? If he's really cute, then say whatever you want to say! That's what you've always done before, right?

Ellie

CHAPTER 4
An Honest Effort

Finally, Maria thought as the bell rang. She threw her history book in her bag and was the first person out of the classroom. She hadn't been able to stop seething all class over the scene Ken had pulled with that girl. Was that his way of trying to win her back? At this point she really didn't care, and she wanted to make sure that he knew that too.

She barreled down the hallway, determined to make sure Ken couldn't keep up with her if that was his goal. But when she glanced over her shoulder, she saw him chasing after her.

"Maria!" he called, seeming to leap over the few people behind her in the hallway. Maria had forgotten that he was a football player.

Used to knocking people over, she thought. If Ken were just the same guy she fell for in the beginning, she probably wouldn't have to be convinced to forgive him right now.

"Maria, stop!" Ken called out, now at her elbow.

Maria whirled around to face Ken. The smile quickly faded from his face when he saw her scowl.

"What is it, Ken?" she snapped.

Ken pulled her over to the side of the busy hallway. "I just wanted to tell you that what you saw before, in class, it wasn't anything," he babbled. "I was only talking to Abby because I had nothing else to do. I was killing time before class, and since you weren't talking to me . . ."

"What are you saying?" Maria demanded. "Somehow your flirting is my fault? I can't believe you. Are you really willing to just go after whoever's there at the moment? You use that girl in class and you date Melissa just because you feel sorry for her? Because she was there and lonely?"

Ken's face paled, and Maria felt a twinge of guilt for being so harsh. But *he* was the one acting like an idiot here!

"No, I know what I want," Ken said, his eyes pleading with her.

"How do I know I'm not just another one of these girls you use to get what you want?" she asked. "And then when you're tired of me or when there's a big football party going on, it's bye-bye, Maria."

"Maria, *no,*" he said, his tone firm. "I know I didn't say this very well last night—I'm not great with words, and you know that. But you're the one I want. No one else matters."

Maria bit her lip, trying not to feel the way her heart was completely melting at his words. He did seem to really care about getting her to understand.

Then out of the corner of her eye Maria caught sight of Melissa and her friends walking down the hallway. Melissa's ice blue eyes seemed to burn a hole right through Maria, making her shudder. And then it hit her all over again—the pain of seeing Ken with that witch, wondering who he could even be anymore if he could date someone like her.

Maria clenched and unclenched her hands and took a deep breath. "Look, Ken, I don't care how many cute girls you flirt with—or even date for that matter. We're over," she said forcefully. "And we're not getting back together."

She steeled herself to the pain she saw in Ken's eyes, reminding herself that he wasn't *her* Ken anymore. He was a guy who cared more about football and winning than who he even dated. Before he could respond, she turned and rushed off. This time he didn't go after her.

She made it as far as the girls' bathroom before she nearly dissolved into tears. She pushed open the heavy door, hoping she wouldn't run into anyone—

especially Melissa. Luckily the bathroom stalls were empty and no one was at the sinks. The overhead fluorescent lights made her squint, but she reached for some paper towels and caught a glimpse of herself in the mirror. Her eyes were rimmed in red, and her cheeks were flushed.

Great! I look really together, she thought.

Maria turned on a faucet and let the water run cool. *How can I keep letting Ken get to me like this? If he could just open his heart and make an honest effort with me. If he could just amazingly morph into the Ken he used to be . . .*

She splashed the cool water on her face, letting it run down to her neck before she reached for more paper towels. She looked in the mirror again and took a deep breath.

Maria, pull it together, she thought. It really didn't look like she and Ken were ever going to be a couple again. And that was what she'd decided. So why did it still hurt so badly?

"So do you want any of my fries?" Jade asked Evan.

"Nope," Evan replied.

"You'll just take them while I'm not looking, right?" Jade teased. She kicked him under the table, and they both laughed. Jade flicked her shoulder-length black hair back from her face, then popped one of the fries in her mouth.

The cafeteria was filled with hungry second-period lunchers, but Jade didn't notice anyone else. Evan was amazing. Jade couldn't remember ever being this happy with anyone, even Jeremy. With Jeremy it was like a part of her felt she had to try really hard somehow—to make him happy, to deserve him. But with Evan everything was just fun. The way it was supposed to be.

And more. Evan was fun, but he was also an incredibly good flirt and a great listener. *Maybe too great,* she thought, wiping a dab of ketchup off her chin. It was fine when she was the one who needed to talk, but did he have to be the whole world's best friend? Couldn't people like Elizabeth Wakefield—for instance—find someone else to listen to their problems?

"So, you still want to see that movie tomorrow?" Jade asked, reminding herself that she was the one who got to be alone with him.

"You're not backing out, are you?" Evan asked as he picked at his veggie pita sandwich and eyed her french fries.

"What? No way. I love Adam Sandler. His movies just keep getting funnier and funnier," she said.

"I don't know," Evan said. "That last one was kind of cheesy."

"That's the point," Jade said, tossing a fry onto Evan's plate. "He's a cheesy comedian. That's what's great about him."

"Speaking of cheese, how come you never get the cheese fries?" he asked. He picked up the french fry on his plate and leaned over to dip it in her ketchup.

"Oh, so you can eat them all?" she joked. "I don't think so."

Evan laughed, and Jade started to giggle too.

"Hey."

Jade stopped laughing and looked up, afraid she knew exactly whose voice that was. Yep—she was right. Elizabeth was standing at their table. She looked even worse than she had last night—like the tears were going to start flowing any minute.

"Liz! Are you okay?" Evan asked immediately. "Sit down," he said, scooting his chair over so Elizabeth could pull up a seat between him and Jade.

Jade couldn't believe Elizabeth was doing her whole damsel-in-distress act again. Didn't Elizabeth have other friends to turn to, like her twin sister for one? Why was Evan always the one she came to with her problems?

Elizabeth plopped down in the seat, turning her back on Jade and facing Evan. "I just came from the *Oracle* office," she said, her voice shaky. "Conner finally told me who that girl was last night. Her name is Alanna, and she and Conner hooked up while he was in rehab."

Jade's eyes opened a little wider. She couldn't believe the way Elizabeth told Evan all her personal problems. This was some great gossip, but for once she didn't care about that. She wanted to know how long this was going to go on—Elizabeth running to Evan every time something went wrong with Conner. She wanted to feel sorry for the girl that her kind-of boyfriend cheated on her, but she was way too close to telling her to lay off *her* boyfriend.

"Actually, I already knew about Alanna," Evan said quietly.

"You did?" Elizabeth asked.

You did? Jade echoed inside. Once again she'd been left in the cold. Why hadn't Evan told her any of that? Wasn't that the kind of stuff you told your girlfriend—especially when she'd sat through a whole car ride of hearing about another girl's problems?

Of course, Evan did have this knack for forgetting Jade existed once Elizabeth entered the picture. Maybe that was the problem. Jade sighed and took a bite of her sandwich.

"I knew about her because Conner told me, but I didn't think it was right for me to say anything to you," Evan explained. "I mean, I wasn't telling him about . . . about us. Because you asked me not to. You wanted him to hear it from you. And I figured this was something *you* should hear from *him*."

"Yeah, I guess I understand," Elizabeth said, sounding defeated.

Jade couldn't believe this. Now he was sitting there making references to "us"—as in him and Elizabeth, not him and *her*—right in front of Jade. She had to get out of here.

Jade jumped up, then reached down to grab her backpack. "Well, I'm done eating," she announced a little louder than necessary. "I have a trig test next period, and I need to cram a few pages of notes before then," she said, wondering why she was even bothering to offer an explanation. No one seemed to be listening.

Evan leaned around Elizabeth. "Good luck," he told her with his trademark grin. "I'll see you later."

"Yeah, see you," she said. She turned and rushed away. When she got to the double doors of the cafeteria, Jade turned in time to see Evan put his hand on Elizabeth's back. If she didn't know any better, from here she would have thought they were a couple.

Jade didn't have a trig test to study for, but she did have something to find out. She needed to know exactly what went on between Evan and Elizabeth. It seemed like it was a whole lot more complicated than just that one kiss at the homecoming dance she'd seen.

Luckily Jade knew just who to ask. She took off down the hall, her platforms clicking on the floor as she ran. She needed to find Jessica.

Will moved past the empty classrooms on his crutches, relieved that the hallway was totally deserted. He still couldn't deal with people watching him hobble around. It was lunchtime, but Will wasn't exactly hungry. Knowing that he had to meet with his parents and Nelson had his stomach tied in knots.

He'd hoped that talking to Coach Riley would somehow magically make everything better—but unfortunately he just felt more confused than ever. He had never imagined himself as a coach. He tried to picture himself as one now—calling plays and inspiring his players with words of wisdom, giving advice from his own glory days. Maybe it wouldn't really be that bad. He did love being on the field. At least he had an option that involved football.

And it might reassure his parents to show that he'd been thinking about this stuff. He could bring up the coaching idea for now just to keep everyone satisfied. He only hoped they didn't ask him why he wanted to be a coach because he hadn't thought it through that much yet.

Suddenly the silence of the hallway was interrupted by female giggles coming toward him. Will glanced up in time to see Melissa and some of her friends, including Cherie Reese, rounding the corner. He caught something about a party that Cherie was planning for Saturday night.

"Of course they can bring beer if they want. I'm just not going to pay Heather's older brother extra to go get it," Cherie said.

"Maybe he'll do it for—" Melissa broke off her sentence when she saw Will. "I'll see you guys later," she told her friends. Then she quickly hurried over to him.

"Will, hey," she said, her voice brighter than usual. He looked back at her friends, who were already walking away. They used to treat him like a god, but now that he wasn't a star football player anymore, he didn't seem to rate on their radar, even if he was involved with their "leader," Melissa.

"Hey," Will said, giving her a slight nod.

"Are you all right?" Melissa asked once her friends were out of earshot. She stepped closer to him, putting her hand on his arm. "What's wrong?"

He kept forgetting that just like he knew Melissa inside out—she could read him without even trying.

"It's no big deal," he hedged, still wondering if letting her back in his life was the best idea.

"Will, come on," she said. She pushed a few strands of brown hair out of her face, focusing her blue eyes directly on his. "You can tell me," she said softly.

Why did he even try to resist her? Melissa would never be out of his system. At least she cared. That was something.

"Last night when I got home, my parents ambushed me," he said, leaning back against the wall for support. "They wanted to talk about my future. Actually, the fact that I don't have one." He sighed. "Anyway, they set up an appointment for this afternoon with Nelson."

"Oh, the dreaded 'talk,'" Melissa said. "Don't worry. It'll blow over as soon as you get into a college."

"Yeah, maybe, but I've been thinking about it a lot too, Liss," he said. "I went to Coach Riley to talk about stuff. He had this idea about what I could do. He said maybe I should be a coach, like him. I mean, I know it's pretty lame and all, but it's something, right?"

He looked down at Melissa hopefully, waiting for her to say that it wasn't lame at all—it was a great idea, and it would solve everything.

Instead her jaw dropped. "You as a *coach?*" she

said, her voice dripping with revulsion. Will winced. "Will, you can't go from being a star player to some washed-up old coach," she continued. "Some life that would be. Besides, high-school football coaches make no money and they get *zero* respect."

Will felt like he had just been flattened by a truck. He knew that it wasn't a very glamorous job, but at this point he wasn't in a situation to be picky as far as his future was concerned. He had hoped that Melissa would at least be glad that he was thinking about things.

"Look, Will, I don't mean to shoot down your idea—I mean, Coach Riley's idea—but things will get better," Melissa said, hardening her gaze. "You don't have to turn into a football coach just yet. There have to be better options than that."

Will felt his face grow hot. Not that he would ever cry—especially not in front of Melissa. But being told by his ex-girlfriend—maybe girlfriend again—that he was a loser with nothing to look forward to wasn't something he could handle right now.

The hall was starting to fill with students, and Will realized lunch was going to be over soon.

Melissa squeezed his arm, giving him a smile that somehow seemed totally cold. "Don't look so *defeated*," she told him. "We'll figure things out later, okay?" She reached up on her tiptoes and kissed him on the cheek. "I have to run, but we'll talk more, I promise. And good luck in the meeting!" With that, she turned and pranced away, as if this whole conversation hadn't bothered her at all.

Why would it? Melissa wasn't the one with the dead-end life.

Jade scanned the quad. The early morning drizzle had burned off into a beautiful afternoon, and there were happy couples smiling and laughing everywhere. It only made her wish she were with Evan right now. That's why she was there, though—to fix her relationship with Evan.

She spotted Jessica sitting all alone in the shade of a tree, studying her notes. Jessica, studying? That was weird. *She must actually* have *a test,* Jade thought, remembering the lie she'd told Evan.

Jade thought about leaving Jessica alone, in case she really needed to cram. But Jade had to know the truth about Elizabeth and Evan, and Jessica of all people would get how important that was. Jessica wasn't one of those annoying people who thought school was the most important thing in your life. *Although her sister is,* Jade couldn't help thinking. Yet somehow Elizabeth *still* had guys crawling all over her. Evan seemed to drop everything when Elizabeth needed help—even Jade. If she wanted to stay in control of things, she needed all the background information on the two of them.

Jade walked over to Jessica, who didn't even look up from her notebook. "Hey!" Jade said, shielding her eyes from the bright California sunshine. She was sorry she had left her sunglasses in her locker. She could hardly see anything out here.

Jessica jerked up her head, obviously surprised. "Oh, hey, Jade," she said. "What's up?"

"Um, I was wondering if I could talk to you for a minute," Jade said. "Do you have time?" she asked, pointing at Jessica's notebook.

"Oh, yeah," Jessica said, closing the book. "There's not much more you can learn two minutes before the test anyway," she said with a shrug.

"Yeah, I know what you mean." Jade plopped down next to her, sitting on her heels.

"So what's going on?" Jessica asked.

Jade bit her lip. "I, um, I just witnessed a pretty personal conversation between Evan and Liz," she said. "We were—Evan and I, I mean—we were eating lunch in the cafeteria, and then Elizabeth showed up and started pouring out all this stuff about Conner. And then . . . they started talking about what happened between *them*—like, this secret they had from Conner or whatever." Jade took a deep breath. "I saw Evan and Liz kiss at the homecoming dance, but it seems like there's more. I know she's your sister, but since Evan and I are together now, it just seems like I should know what the deal is."

Jade sat up straighter, ready to take whatever Jessica was about to tell her. She hoped it was that she was reading too much into it, and that was all there was to it.

Jessica pulled her legs close up under her chin. "Well, Liz never told me not to talk about this with anyone besides Conner," she said. She laughed to herself. "As if Conner and I could ever have a normal conversation anyway," she added, shaking her head. "But yeah, I can tell you what I know. Basically, nothing much really happened between them. But Evan *was* really hung up on her. He'd liked her even before he went out with me. Sometimes I wonder if he only went out with me because he couldn't have her."

Jade cringed. She knew that feeling all too well.

"So, once Conner seemed out of the picture, Evan made his move," Jessica went on. "And I think he pushed pretty hard. He even asked me to help. They had this whole should-we-or-shouldn't-we? thing going on for a couple of weeks. They went out on a couple of dates. But Liz just wasn't into it. For whatever reasons, she can't see anyone but Conner."

Jade felt herself slump. She couldn't believe it. So Evan and Elizabeth did have more going on than just a kiss at the homecoming dance. And if Jessica thought *she* had been second pick for him, then it was probably the same thing with Jade. Now that Conner and Elizabeth were done, then maybe Elizabeth would change her mind about Evan. And from what Jessica was saying, that would mean Jade would be out the door.

Suddenly the bright sunshine that had been warming Jade's back moved under a cloud. She shivered, pulled her violet cardigan sweater tighter around her.

"Are you okay?" Jessica asked, gathering up her books from the blanket and stuffing them into her backpack. "I mean, I don't want to give you the wrong idea. This is all in the past now. Evan's totally into you—it's obvious."

Jade forced a smile, appreciating Jessica's effort to make her feel better. "Uh, yeah, I'm fine," she lied. "I guess I just didn't know that Evan had liked your sister that much."

Jessica checked the ground for anything she'd forgotten and grabbed a pen she found lying a couple of feet away. Around them everyone else was packing up too, anticipating the bell that would ring any second.

Jade was perfectly happy to get out of here and go to class. At least it would be a distraction from all the bad news she'd just gotten. She let her hair fall over her face to keep Jessica from seeing just how upset she was.

"Well, thanks for filling me in," Jade said, standing up. "And good luck on your test!"

"Thanks. I'll see you at cheerleading," Jessica said, already moving toward the school's bright blue double doors.

Jade hung back and watched the quad empty. She felt like the wind had just been knocked out of her. What was it with these Wakefield twins and the hold they had over the guys she dated?

Melissa Fox

Will,

Hi! I just wanted to let you know that I'll be thinking about you this afternoon when you're in your meeting. It's really all going to turn out okay for us, I'm sure. Of course that whole coaching idea is a joke, and I know you think so too. But we'll figure out something else. I just wanted to let you know that I'll be here, like always. Maybe we can get together sometime this weekend. Dinner at First and Ten? We'll talk more later.

Love,
Liss

To: jaames@cal.rr.com
From: jess1@cal.rr.com
Subject: u & me

Hey, J.!

Do you have any idea how lucky we are? I'm so glad we don't have all kinds of icky secrets from each other. I just wish all my friends could be as happy as I am!

Love,
Jess

Jeremy Aames

Okay, here's the question—what's the exact definition of a secret? It wouldn't, for instance, count as a secret that I didn't tell Jessica about sending away for an application to an archaeology program at a college in Arizona, would it? I mean, I don't tell her every little thing I do every day—like when I brush my teeth or whatever—and that's not keeping secrets. And it's not like I've actually gotten into the school or even applied yet.

I will tell her, at some point. It's just I'm not even sure if archaeology is definitely what I want to do. Well, I'm pretty sure. But what if she thinks I'm a total dork when I tell her that?

I don't think it counts as a secret.

CHAPTER 5 Ready for Battle

Maria walked out of her student-government meeting more tired than she'd felt in a long time. She had already been having one of the longest, worst days of her life before the student representatives decided to bring up just about everything on the agenda for the rest of the school year. The yelling and debating had gone on for more than the scheduled hour.

All she had been able to think about was Ken. She couldn't believe his nerve, but she also couldn't deny that she still had feelings for him. If she didn't, he wouldn't be able to get her so upset.

I guess I can admit my feelings to myself as long as I don't admit them to Ken, she thought.

He was just so frustrating. It was like he couldn't even nail down a good apology, Maria thought as she wandered down the hall to her locker.

She was just so relieved this day was finally over. She opened her locker and started pulling out the books that she'd need for her homework that night.

Calc, chem, her paperback copy of *Emma* for English-lit class, her scene for drama.

Maria was so lost in thought, she almost didn't even hear the male voice calling her name. Then it sank in.

Ken!

For a moment Maria's heart skipped a beat, and her breath caught in her throat. She stared into her locker, wondering if she should turn around and face him.

No. Maria wasn't about to forgive him. She had to remember why they weren't together anymore. He had hurt her, really badly.

"Maria!" The voice sounded so insistent—and she realized now that it wasn't Ken.

Good, she thought, even though her shoulders slumped a little.

Maria peered out from her locker and slammed it shut. It was Steve, the student-council vice president. Steve, the National Honor Society treasurer, the cocaptain of the rugby team, and the guy she had had a crush on sophomore year. He had totally been Maria's type—before Ken.

"Hey, Steve," she said.

He reached her locker and flashed a friendly smile. "I was calling your name for a while. Everything okay?" he asked.

"Yeah, I'm just trying to clear my head from all the voices in that meeting," she said. "I must have spaced and thought you were someone *else* disagreeing with my ideas for the Christmas dance!"

Steve's grin widened. The skin near his eyes wrinkled, just like Ken's did when he smiled. Why couldn't she get Ken out of her mind?

"It did turn into a yelling match, didn't it?" he asked, leaning against the row of orange lockers. "Who knew a holiday dance could get people so emotional?"

"Tell me about it," Maria said, rolling her eyes. "Was it really necessary that we go thirty-five minutes over to hear Matt Maxwell and Kevin Clark argue over the color of the streamers?"

"Yeah, those guys are brutal when they disagree," Steve replied. "I could sure use a night of relaxation."

A night of relaxation sounded perfect to Maria. She could take a bubble bath and listen to some music. Anything to get her mind off Ken for a few minutes. She'd indulge right after she worked on her drama scene a little more.

"Hey," Steve interrupted her thoughts. "Would you be interested in getting that cup of coffee you promised me a while ago? We could go in like a couple of hours?" he asked, leaning forward slightly. His brown eyes sparkled.

Maria felt her cheeks redden slightly. She knew she should say yes and try to get Ken out of her head once and for all. Steve was smart, cute, and always so nice to her. He also seemed honest—which was rare for a guy interested in politics. *Make that any guy.* If Ken were only honest, she wouldn't be in this position of trying to decide whether to accept a date with some other guy.

Ugh! Here I am talking to a great, single guy who is obviously interested in me, and all I can think about is Ken. Obviously a date so soon was a bad idea.

A classroom door opened, and a couple of students walked out. Maria glanced over to see Ken standing there, watching her and Steve, a strange look of confusion on his face.

Maria felt her face get even warmer. Suddenly all she could think about was Ken flirting with Abby Carter and dating Melissa Fox. She had to get over him—and a date with Steve would be a good way to force her to forget Ken.

Maria turned her gaze back to Steve and gave him what she hoped was a dazzling smile. "I would love to get a cup of coffee with you," Maria said. She felt herself speaking just a little louder but told herself it was so Steve could hear her better over all the noise in the hallway.

"Great!" Steve said. He didn't even notice that

Maria was looking over his shoulder, dividing her attention between him and Ken. Out of the corner of her eye she watched Ken move down the hallway.

He looked like he'd just learned he wasn't going to graduate from high school. He didn't meet Maria's gaze, and his shoulders were slumped toward the ground. He reminded Maria of a wounded puppy.

"I'll meet you at House of Java around six," Steve said, shifting his backpack from one shoulder to the other. "It'll be nice to unwind." He gave her a wink and took off in the opposite direction than Ken had taken.

Maria turned around to see if Ken was still there, watching. But the hallway was empty.

It's time to move on. Ken and I are over, and Steve is just the right guy to help me forget about him, she thought.

She pictured Steve's curly black hair and easygoing smile. Finally she had found her answer to getting over Ken Matthews.

Will couldn't believe the day was finally over. It had flown by, but only because he was dreading what came at the end—the meeting with his parents and Mr. Nelson. Unfortunately, since Melissa had blown a hole in Coach Riley's idea and Will couldn't come up with anything else, he was showing up without any ideas to present to his parents and Nelson.

He had never wanted a school day to last longer so much before. Even another helping of calculus class was more appealing than this meeting.

As he approached Nelson's office on his crutches, he saw his parents sitting on the bench outside the door. They had the same expressions on their faces that they had had the night before. They looked ready for battle. Only this battle was pretty unfair. It was three against one.

Will had a sinking feeling that this meeting wasn't going to end well. His conversation with Melissa hadn't pumped him full of hope either. Why did she have to be so down on the idea of him being a football coach? Yeah, at first he hadn't liked it. But after thinking it over, he'd realized that it seemed as good an idea as any. And he was looking for *any* idea right now.

For a moment Will considered turning around and walking the other way. What would be the harm in missing only the most important meeting of his high-school career?

"Hi, Will," his mom called, rising from the bench while she smoothed her suit skirt.

"How was your day?" his dad asked, walking toward him.

Horrible because I was dreading this moment, he thought about saying as he approached them. Instead he mumbled a "fine" and sat down a little too hard on the bench.

"How long have you been here?" he asked, staring at the linoleum-tile floor.

"Just a few minutes," his dad answered. "We left work a little early."

Now his parents were leaving work early to deal with his problems—their problem son. He could imagine them each going to their bosses and asking to leave early because their son didn't know what he was doing with his life.

This whole experience was utterly humiliating.

Mr. Nelson opened the door to his office. "Mr. and Mrs. Simmons?" he asked.

Will's parents nodded, and Mr. Nelson ushered them in. He shook both of their hands.

"Hello. Sorry to keep you waiting," he said. "Hi, Will," he added, almost as an afterthought.

Mr. Nelson's small office was crammed full of catalogs and brochures from various colleges. It was intimidating just looking at all of the college posters that lined the wall. The schools were all lush and green with ivy-covered walls, impressive stone buildings, and perfect, smiling students. Will's stomach lurched as he saw one for the University of Michigan.

His life could have been perfect right now. He could have his early acceptance letter to U of Mich and be kicking back right now, coasting happily through senior year. What he had always imagined would be the best year of his life.

"So," Mr. Nelson said, opening a thick folder and staring at the papers inside. "We're here to discuss Will and his future."

Will gaped, wondering what was inside that file—it was huge. Did that cover the whole senior class or just him?

"So, you had been planning on the University of Michigan, right?" Mr. Nelson asked, removing his horn-rimmed glasses and glancing in Will's direction.

Will nodded and slumped slightly in his seat. Why did Nelson have to even bring it up? They all knew it was out of the question now.

Mr. Nelson glanced down at what Will assumed was his transcript. "Hmmm . . . ," he said.

Will looked over nervously at his parents just as they glanced in his direction. His mother gave him a small, reassuring smile. *A smile of pity,* Will thought.

"Michigan may be a bit of a stretch for you now that you're no longer an athlete," Mr. Nelson said. "But there are plenty of other schools that would be happy to have him," he added, focusing his attention on Will's parents.

They were talking about him as if he wasn't even sitting there. Maybe the three of them would like to have this meeting alone—without him? He'd be more than happy to make that possible and get up and leave. Will wished he was anywhere but here right now.

"Your grades are solid enough to get into a decent school," Mr. Nelson continued, turning back to Will. At least he was recognizing that it was Will's future and his decision to make. "But I'm a little concerned that you show some ambition and motivation in the process, Will. Other senior students have sent out all their applications, and many have been here to talk to me on their own—without their parents."

Will sagged down a little further in his seat.

"Do you know what you want to do? Many freshmen change their major, but if you're set on a career, you can base your college choice in part on a school that's known for accounting or medicine or education," Mr. Nelson said, leaning back in his big leather chair. "Are there any talents you'd like to develop?"

Will felt all three sets of eyes on him, burning into him. Having his parents on his case was enough, but now Nelson was on their side. He felt the lump in his throat getting bigger.

"I—I don't know. I can't think of any—right

now," Will choked out, staring down at the floor. Why couldn't they all just leave him alone?

Mr. Nelson and his parents exchanged worried glances.

Great. Will shook his head, kicking at the peeling carpet with his good foot. He was only seventeen and already a miserable failure.

"Matthews! Get your head in the game!" shouted Coach Riley. "Look for the open man and aim!" Coach's arms flailed, and he grabbed the playbook off the bench.

The air was crisp and cool. It was Ken's favorite kind of football weather, but he just couldn't concentrate on today's intense practice. Coach Riley was really putting the guys through their paces. They'd already done sprints, and now he was working on passing.

Normally passing—finding an open man and hurling the ball as hard as he could—was one of Ken's favorite parts of practice. It usually helped clear his mind, but today all he could think about was Maria.

He couldn't believe she had accepted a date with that Steve jerk right in front of him. Okay, so maybe that was her way of getting back at him after the Abby thing, but at least he hadn't asked Abby out right in front of Maria. What else could he do to convince Maria that they belonged together?

Ken brought his arm back automatically and completely overthrew his shot, missing the open man in the end zone and nearly hitting the goalpost. He was channeling all his aggression into the football.

Ken tried to shake the feeling that he was watching someone else play football. His arm and his head were definitely not working together today.

"You okay, Ken?" Todd Wilkins jogged over to him and slapped him on the back. "You seem kind of spaced today."

"Yeah, but I'm all right. Get back out there and I'll send you something," Ken said, tossing the football into the air.

"That's the Matthews I know," Todd said, trotting off down the field.

When he got to the other end of the field, Todd signaled he was ready to receive. Ken pulled back his arm and thought about how he'd like to launch Mr. VP Steve across the field just like this ball.

The second the ball left his hands, Ken knew that this pass was even worse than the last. It spiked in the air and came crashing down yards before any of the receivers.

"Good one!" shouted Matt Wells. Two other receivers clapped and hooted.

Ken scowled.

"Matthews, we're playing football, not badminton!" Coach Riley yelled.

Ken knew he should care that he was flubbing almost every play, but he really didn't. He could only think of Maria. Right now she was probably getting ready for her date with Steve.

He imagined her picking out an outfit, maybe those khaki pants with that black cropped turtleneck that showed just a flash of her stomach. Ken always loved her in that.

His palms were sweating. He wiped them on his jersey and ran a hand through his wet hair. Would this practice ever end?

Coach Riley finally blew his whistle, a look of disgust on his face that Ken could see from midfield.

"That was a pretty weak play," Coach Riley said as Ken made his way to the bench for a drink of water.

"Sorry, Coach. I'll be back in the game tomorrow, I promise," Ken said, taking off his helmet.

"Hit the showers, Matthews," he mumbled, shaking his head.

Ken knew he should be more upset. Normally a practice like the one he had just had would inspire him to stay late and try to make up for it. But he knew he wouldn't be able to get his "head in the game," as Coach liked to say. He just didn't care about football right now.

However, judging from the looks of Wilkins, Rumsey, and the other players heading his way, he was the only one who didn't care. They had "we need to talk" written all over their grim faces.

"Matthews, you really sucked out there today," Rumsey said.

"Yeah, I know." Ken shrugged. He started walking toward the locker room, and the others followed alongside him. "I've just got a lot going on right now. I had some trouble concentrating," he said, aware that it was a lame excuse.

"Well, if you need to talk, your teammates are always here for you—even if your passes aren't there for them," Todd said, giving him a shove toward the lockers.

"Thanks a lot," Ken grumbled sarcastically. He opened his locker and peeled off his shoulder pads.

Maybe Todd was right, though. Maybe he could ask them for advice. Lots of the guys on the team had girlfriends, and they'd all had girl problems in the past. He should talk to them, tell them what was happening with Maria right now. He might even get some decent advice. It couldn't hurt—and it just might help.

After all, Maria was hardly talking to him. Right

now she was probably flirting with Steve over a vanilla latte at House of Java—the place where she'd royally blown Ken off the night before.

Ken sat down on the bench and began unlacing his dirt-encrusted cleats. One thing was for sure, he needed to fix everything with Maria or he was going to go crazy—and his football career might come to a quick end too.

To: lizw@cal.rr.com
From: mslater@swiftnet.com
Subject: Ah!

Hi, Liz! I just wanted to thank you for listening to me last night. These guys are driving both of us crazy. Today in class Ken flirted like crazy with Abby Carter. He'd never said a word to her before! I guess he was trying to get my attention or something, but I just got angry at him. The Ken I went out with would never have pulled something so dumb, you know?

Then after the student-council meeting Steve asked me out. I was going to say no, but I saw Ken coming down the hall and I couldn't stop myself—I told Steve I'd go with him to HOJ for a cup of coffee.

Liz, you should have seen the look on Ken's face when he overheard. But I can't sit around forever waiting for Ken to get his act together, right? Right?

CHAPTER 6

Plan B

Your first date since the breakup, Maria thought as she strode toward the door of House of Java. She had taken extra time getting ready, and she knew she looked good. She had finally decided to go with her nice khaki pants and the black turtleneck Ken had always liked. She had even put on some makeup—more than her usual light lip gloss—and spritzed on some perfume. Ken—*Steve*—would definitely approve.

Of course, when they were together, Ken had liked most of what she wore. He was always telling her how beautiful she looked.

Maria shook her head. She just needed to get through this date without wimping out and without thinking about Ken.

She caught sight of her reflection in the door and took a deep breath. *Here goes nothing,* she thought. She opened the door and scanned the room for Steve. He caught her eye, stood up, and waved her over. Maria noticed that his smile got bigger as she got closer. Obviously he thought she looked nice too.

Maria might look good, but she felt awful. She couldn't erase the image of the expression on Ken's face after she accepted the date with Steve. Why did he still have this effect on her after everything he'd pulled?

"Hi," Steve greeted her as he pulled out her chair.

"Hey," Maria answered, mustering up as much enthusiasm as she could. She sat down, carefully crossing her long legs.

"So, I always get the same thing," Steve said. "Do you know what you want, or do you want to come to the counter with me and check out the menu board?" he asked, raising his eyebrows questioningly.

Maria met his gaze—then broke away. "Um, I'll have a tall vanilla latte," she said.

"Great," he said. "Be right back." He got up and walked over to the counter. Maria watched him leave. Steve somehow managed to look casual and put together at the same time. Like right now he had on faded jeans and a nice rugby shirt.

Maria sighed and looked around the coffee shop. House of Java was at a dinnertime lull, but she knew the place would be full again in a couple of hours. Maria glanced back toward the booth where she usually studied on Wednesday nights. It was empty. But the memory of sitting there last night was still fresh in her mind. Why had Ken messed up what was supposed to be an apology?

"She said she'd bring it right over," Steve said, startling Maria and pulling her out of her thoughts. "Everything okay?" he asked, sitting down again.

"Yeah—sure," Maria said. She managed a smile.

The waitress was coming toward them, her hands full of steaming mugs. At least Jessica wasn't on duty tonight. It would have been way too weird going on this date in front of her friend.

"Thanks," Steve said as the waitress placed the drinks on the table in between them. He smiled at Maria. "Smells great, huh?" he asked.

Maria felt like her smile was plastered on her face. Steve was a nice guy. So far he'd been a total gentleman that night, pulling out her chair, asking her what she'd like to order and then going to the counter—the complete opposite of an arrogant football player.

Too bad she knew that everything that night was going to remind her of Ken. Steve had ordered hazelnut coffee. Maria could smell it. Ken's favorite coffee was hazelnut too.

But now that the coffee was here, Maria was determined to forget about Ken. Even though the smell was a powerful reminder.

"There's this great coffee shop right around the corner from my brother's dorm," Steve said, wrapping his hands around his mug. "He goes to college in New York City, so I guess there's probably a million great coffee shops there. But Ken and I went to this one right after I dragged him to see a show one night, and it was really cool."

Maria's breath caught. Had Steve just said his older brother's name was Ken? Or was she just imagining things?

"So, your brother's name is Ken?" she asked, her voice catching.

"Yeah," Steve said with a slight frown. He was obviously confused about why that was the part of his statement she found interesting.

Unbelievable, Maria thought. *His brother's name just had to be Ken.*

"And you've been to a Broadway show?" Maria asked, trying to save the conversation. She did want to hear about the show. She was fascinated by live theater—especially anything performed in New York, the home of Broadway.

Steve nodded. "Actually, I've seen three," he said, lifting his steaming mug and blowing on his coffee. He put it down and tore open two sugar packets, pouring the contents inside his mug.

"Wow! Three Broadway shows," Maria said wistfully. "I've always wanted to go see a play in New York. I hear they're amazing."

"New York is incredible," Steve said, stirring his coffee.

Maria took a sip of her latte and wiped her upper lip with her napkin. So Steve liked theater—they had something in common. That was good. Plus she already knew they were both into student government. That was two things right there.

"I'm actually thinking about going to school there," Steve said. "I used to think I might be an actor, but I've heard it's really hard to do."

"You wanted to be an actor? I thought you wanted to be a politician," Maria said.

"Well, yeah, that's what I want now," Steve said. "But when I was a kid, I had this whole dream about acting." He shrugged. "It probably sounds silly," he muttered.

"No—not at all," Maria said. "Actually, that's really weird. I was an actress when I was younger, and that's why I still do drama. But I pretty much came to the same decision, that I'd rather go for a more solid career. The acting's pretty much a side thing now."

"Wow, cool," Steve said. "So what are you doing in drama class?"

Maria gulped down her sip of latte. "We're actually working on our own interpretations of major scenes," she explained. "I'm doing the love scene between Tony and Maria from *West Side Story.*"

"Great show," Steve said.

"Yeah, I'm almost done writing mine. It's just hard to change something that's already so perfect, you know?"

Steve nodded, smiling. "So you're doing prelaw at college next year, right?" he asked. "I think that's what you said in the interview for the Senate scholarship."

"Yeah, that's the plan," she said, remembering that Steve had been one of the student judges who had probably helped her win the scholarship. Of course, Ken had been on the board too. . . . "But college seems so far off," she continued. "I have to keep reminding myself that this time next year, we'll have graduated and be in our first semester at college."

A group of junior-high kids came through the doors of HOJ. They were pretty noisy, giggling and shouting to each other even though they were standing in a tight group.

"I can't wait to be there," Steve said. He glanced over at the younger kids. "I won't miss this kind of stuff," he added. "Can't they keep it down?" He shook his head.

"I'm excited to graduate but a little sad too," Maria said, staring at the group of kids. They seemed like they were having so much fun.

"Why?" Steve asked. "It's time to get out of Sweet

Valley. I can tell you've got too much going on to stay in this tiny town, Maria."

Maria cringed. She loved Sweet Valley and hated it when people put it down. She and Ken always agreed on that.

You're not here with Ken; you're here with Steve, she reminded herself. And Steve was perfect for her—just the kind of guy she needed to get over Ken.

She polished off her latte and put the glass mug on the table.

"Want another?" Steve asked, finishing off his own coffee.

"No, thanks. It was great, though," Maria said.

"Mind if I have another?" Steve asked, getting up.

"No, that's fine," she said.

Steve walked back toward the counter, and Maria let her forced smile fade. She kept seeing reasons why Steve was good for her, but she just didn't feel that spark she had with Ken. Still, that spark had turned out to mean nothing anyway.

I wonder what Ken is doing right now, she thought. *Probably knocking heads with his fellow football lunkheads.*

She looked up. Steve was back with a full mug of hazelnut. The smell was really throwing her. All she could do was think about Ken.

"I can't get enough of this stuff," he said, sitting down and immediately starting to empty cream and sugar into his mug. "So, I'm sure I can polish this off in the next few minutes. Do you feel like going to take a walk on the beach when I'm done?"

The beach—this was turning into a real date. Coffee was one thing, but a romantic walk on the beach was another.

"I—um," Maria stammered.

"If you have a lot of homework, we can go some other time," he offered.

Maria shook her head. "No, I'm fine with homework," she said. What was her problem? Hadn't she *wanted* this to be a real date? "Sure, the beach sounds great."

Steve grinned and gulped down his coffee a little faster than he had his last cup.

Ken stepped out of the shower and grabbed his towel. He only hoped he hadn't taken too long. He wanted to talk with Todd and the other guys before they headed home.

He had stood under the stream of water for so long that he was pretty waterlogged. He just couldn't stop racking his brain for a way to get Maria interested.

He dried off and reached for his clothes. Maria had been on his mind all day, and if he didn't get some advice on what to do, he had a feeling he wasn't going to sleep that night.

He could hear some guys out in the hall, so Ken threw on his button-down shirt and tucked it into his jeans.

"Hey, Matthews! Are you coming or what?" Todd asked, bursting into the locker room. "You sure took a while in the shower," he said. "Some of the guys are going out for pizza. Wanna come?"

"Nah, I gotta get home," Ken said.

Todd shrugged. "Okay," he said, moving toward the door.

"Hey, um, Todd?" Ken asked.

"Yeah," Todd said, turning back around.

"Can I talk to you for a second?"

"Is this about your horrible play today?" Todd asked.

"It has to do with that, yeah," Ken said, tying his sneakers.

"Shoot!" Todd said, throwing himself down on the bench opposite Ken.

Ken swallowed. *What am I supposed to say? What do I do when I can't get a girl off my mind? How do I forget about Maria? How do I get her back?*

"I was wondering if I could talk to you about a problem I've been having," Ken started.

Just then the locker-room door burst open and

Jason Rumsey and several other guys walked in.

"Wilkins! We're starving. Are you coming or what?" Jason asked.

"In a minute. We're talking," Todd said over his shoulder.

"What about?" Jason asked, sitting down next to Todd.

"Ken wants some advice," Todd explained.

Everyone's eyes turned to Ken, and he shifted uncomfortably, running a hand through his freshly clean hair. *Great! Now everyone's going to put their two cents in.* It was the ultimate humiliation to sit here and ask a bunch of *guys* for help with his "feelings."

Oh, well, he thought. He might as well spill everything now.

Ken wiped his hands on his jeans. "It's about this girl," he began.

The guys all roared their teasing noises, then settled down.

"I thought you were seeing Melissa," Jason said.

"Yeah, I was. That's the problem. We broke up, and now I just want my ex, Maria, back. We went out before things happened between me and Melissa." Melissa. God, it already seemed impossible to believe he'd ever actually gone out with her. "So I tried to tell Maria we should get back together, but she's just acting like it's all over. I don't know what to do to convince her that we're supposed to be together."

"Maybe it's just done," Jason said. "You have to accept it and move on, man. There are tons of girls in this school who'd want to get hooked up with you anyway."

Ken sighed. This was obviously a mistake. "You don't get it," he pressed. "Maria's the one. I know it, and the thing is—I think she knows it too. She's just still mad at the way things ended between us, and I have to find a way to let her know it won't happen again."

"So what have you done so far?" Todd asked.

Ken frowned. "I thought if she saw me flirt with another girl, she'd be jealous and want me back. But it didn't exactly work out."

"I can't believe you actually did that," Jason said, letting out a laugh. "You really do need advice."

"That one never works." Todd shook his head. "You know what you need to do? You need to pull the old I-can't-live-without-you move."

All the other guys nodded.

"I don't get it," Ken said. "What, like, pretend I'm going to kill myself or something?"

"No, man, not like that," Todd said. He rolled his eyes. "You've got to find a reason to ask for Maria's help with something. Let her know you need her and there's no one else who could do whatever it is. Girls go all over that kind of stuff—when you act like you can't deal without them. You'll be back together in no time. Making out behind the bleachers," he teased.

Ken thought about it for a minute. Yeah, that made sense. He'd ask Maria to help him with something, and then they'd spend time together. Even if she was mad, she wouldn't let him down if she thought he really needed help. After all, when he'd taken the bad tackle in that football game, she'd come running onto the field to make sure he was okay. One thing would lead to another, and they'd be back together.

Ken nodded at Todd, Jason, and the others. "Yeah, okay," he said, smiling slightly. "I'll give it a try."

"Excellent," Todd said, standing up. "Let us know how it works out. We'd stick around and help you with your other problems, like your passing, but we're starving."

"Thanks. Later," Ken said, tossing his towel in the nearby laundry bin. He decided to ignore the last crack about his bad play.

"Later, Matthews! Good luck!" they called.

Ken turned back to his locker and threw his deodorant and comb back inside before locking it up and grabbing his jacket off the bench.

Todd better know what he's talking about, he

thought. His plan B needed to move into action before Maria and Steve became a couple.

Conner sat on his bed, strumming his guitar. He sure had gotten out of practice since he had left for rehab. It felt good to pick up his guitar again and play the chords he knew so well.

His days had been completely filled with sessions, meetings, talk groups, therapies. It was strange to be back to homeroom, pop quizzes, tests, and relationship nightmares.

Now, if he could only get Alanna and Elizabeth out of his mind. Alanna and Elizabeth, Elizabeth and Alanna. They were so different. Conner wished he didn't have to make up his mind.

He and Alanna had so much in common. She'd had a rough time with a dad who couldn't care less about her and a mom who was too messed up to actually take care of her. Her friends had been the ones to push her into rehab, just like with Conner. She was almost like a male version of him. Except she was hot.

On the other hand, he and Elizabeth had this—this *thing.* She was so cheerful and trusting—the complete opposite of Conner. But somehow she kind of rubbed off on him sometimes, made him feel like maybe he could make something of his life with her believing in him. And he really couldn't imagine never kissing her again. But he couldn't picture staying away from Alanna for long either.

He needed to make up his mind soon, he knew. He cared about both of them, and he didn't want to put them through all this. He put his feet up on the bed and his head back on the pillow as he played.

He was rusty, but his rehab experiences might make for a good song. That and this crazy Elizabeth-and-Alanna situation. He'd have to work on some lyrics this weekend.

Maybe he'd call it "Relationship Hell." That pretty much summed up how he was feeling right now.

Not too long ago this was just the kind of thing that would make him grab the bottle of scotch or vodka that he'd kept stashed under his bed. Alcohol had always helped him block out the confusion, the needs of everyone around him.

Alcohol. Conner closed his eyes and imagined the feel of the warm liquid sliding down the back of his throat. He'd feel it burn all the way down to his toes, heating him up from the inside out. His shoulders would relax, and a few minutes later everything would seem much less important and less pressing.

Conner shook his head and sat up slightly on his bed. This was exactly the kind of thinking that got him in trouble. He needed to forget about alcohol. Staying sober was more important than anything—even Alanna and Elizabeth. He couldn't let this stuff drive him back to the worst mistake he'd ever made.

He was stronger than that now anyway. From now on he was going to concentrate on his music and everything else that *didn't* make him want to pick up a drink.

He heard a knock on his door. "Yeah?" he called, putting his guitar aside.

"Conner, can I talk to you?" Megan asked, peering around the door. She was still wearing her soccer uniform, smudged with dirt. She'd probably just gotten back from her game.

"Yeah, Sandy, come in," he said. "I wanted to tell you I'm sorry about what happened in school."

"Really? Well, I hope you apologized to Elizabeth," Megan said, flopping down on the bed. "I only hope she forgives you, like I do."

Conner smiled at his little sister. She was pretty great. But she could also be a little too nosy and stick herself too far into his life.

Conner clasped his hands behind his head. He knew that Megan was trying to find out what he was going to do about the Elizabeth-and-Alanna thing. He wished he had something to tell her. But he was as clueless as she was.

"Look, Sandy, I don't know what I'm going to do, if that's what you're wondering. Yeah, I said I was sorry. But I don't know if we're getting back together, okay?"

Megan's face sagged into a frown. "Oh," she said.

"I know that you and Liz are friends," Conner continued. "But it's not like you can't be friends just because she's not my girlfriend."

"I know," Megan said, getting up. "I'm going to go shower so you can have your precious privacy back," she teased.

Conner gave her a half smile, then picked up his guitar as she wandered out of the room and shut the door behind her.

Now he was in danger of disappointing his little sister too.

It was amazing—the sharpness of the craving. Jeff had warned him about this, how he'd think he was fine and then something would happen and all he'd be able to think about was the way it would feel to take a drink.

It doesn't mean I have to give in, he told himself, picking out a few chords on the guitar. He was done being a coward—a drunk. And he'd find a way to make this decision without any help from alcohol.

Elizabeth Wakefield

So, I know the truth. Conner did the decent thing and told me about this girl. Alanna. I should be happy, right? He's being honest. He even said he was <u>sorry</u> when he realized he was wrong about something. A miracle.

Alanna. What a stupid name.

Okay, I'm not going to pressure him. As badly as I want to call him and say he has to choose me and we belong together, I'm not going to do it. He's gone through too much. I'm going to wait this out—one more time.

If Conner chooses me, this will be the last time I let him have all the power like this. Things will be different between us.

And if he doesn't choose me . . . I'm not even going to think about that.

CHAPTER 7
Coming Clean

"You should be glad you got me out of there before I got a caffeine rush," Steve said cheerfully as he and Maria walked toward his blue Toyota Corolla. Maria's mom had dropped her off at House of Java since Steve had told her he could give her a ride home.

"I don't want to expose you to that side of me too soon and scare you off," he joked. He unlocked the passenger-side door, and Maria slid in.

Okay, I guess he thinks this date is going well, she thought. And it was, by all normal standards. She did a quick check of her makeup in the rearview mirror before Steve reached the driver's side. Lipstick still in place. Lashes still appropriately thick and dark.

Steve got in the car and started up the engine. "So, Crescent Beach?" he asked, looking over toward Maria for approval.

Crescent Beach. Her and Ken's favorite place to go together.

Forget about Ken, she ordered herself. *Have fun tonight.*

"Sure," she answered in a small voice. "Crescent Beach sounds good," she lied.

"Cool," Steve said as he turned on the radio. Maria was silent for the rest of the ride, just relieved that Steve seemed content to listen to the music.

Why did I agree to do this? she wondered, staring down at her hands. Yeah, this was all supposed to help her forget about Ken. But so far it had done the opposite. And besides, was it really fair to Steve to use him like that?

They reached the beach, and Steve pulled into a space in the municipal parking lot near the catamarans. The windows of his car were down, and Maria could see the moonlight reflecting on the water. She inhaled, and salt air filled her lungs. It felt good—cleansing and refreshing. Maybe this *had* been a smart move.

She raised her eyes to the sky and took in the nearly full moon. The beach was the perfect spot to stargaze. The last time she had done that was with Ken.

They had walked along near the water, holding hands and kissing. Then Ken had splashed her with a little water and a full-on water fight had erupted. The weird thing was that even that had been romantic.

They were soaking wet by the time they were done, but Maria remembered feeling so happy, so connected to Ken.

Maria sighed. She knew what she had to do.

Steve came around to open Maria's door, but she didn't make any move to get out of the car. She turned to Steve. He looked confused and a little concerned.

"Is everything okay? Too cold out here?" he asked, starting to take off his jacket to drape around Maria's shoulders.

Maria shook her head. "Steve, I'm sorry. Can you get back in the car?"

Steve's eyebrows shot up in surprise, but he nodded and walked around the car to get back in.

"What's wrong?" he asked, shutting his door. "Do you feel sick?"

Maria swallowed hard. This was harder to do than she'd thought. "N-No," she stammered.

"Maria, whatever it is, it's fine. I've had a great time tonight. We can go home and come to the beach another time."

Maria shook her head. "I'm sorry I didn't tell you this sooner, but I'm still hung up on someone else. The last time I was here was with him," she blurted out.

"Oh, I see," Steve said, unable to hide the disappointment creeping into his voice.

"I'm so sorry," Maria said, turning toward him and making real eye contact for what felt like the first time that night. She could finally be honest with him. "I wanted to get over him, and I did want to go out with you tonight. But I think I need to figure some more things out before we go out again, and tonight isn't really working. It just doesn't seem fair to you."

Steve nodded and put the keys back in the ignition. "I'll get you home," he said, a little tightly.

Maria chewed on her lip. She knew he was disappointed, but she had hoped she might be able to tell him about what was going on—as a friend, so he could understand a little more and maybe even offer some advice, from a guy's perspective. But that was probably asking too much from a guy who thought they had a future together five minutes ago. She only hoped he didn't hate her.

Once he had backed up and pulled out of the lot, Steve glanced over at Maria. "Thanks for being honest," he said. "I noticed you kind of drifting in and out of the conversation tonight."

Maria folded her hands together in her lap. She felt pretty guilty for misleading Steve the way she did. Maybe he didn't want details of the guy she was thinking about, but at least he was being nice.

Luckily the drive from the beach to Maria's house

wasn't too long. They didn't talk, instead relying on the radio to fill the tense silence in the car. Ten minutes later Steve pulled into the Slaters' driveway.

"I still had fun tonight," Maria offered up lamely. "Thanks for the coffee and the conversation."

"Yeah, no problem," Steve said, gripping the wheel. "See you in student council."

Maria waited a second to see if he'd get out of the car and open her door for her again, but Steve didn't move, so she opened the door and climbed out.

Maria couldn't believe she'd ruined what could have been a perfectly good date. She was about as depressed as she'd been all day. And she hadn't thought that would be possible when she first told Steve she'd go out with him.

She slowly made her way up the lawn toward her house. There was only one thing she could do to feel better right now. Coming clean had worked with one guy. She needed to try it on another. Tomorrow she was going to tell Ken how she really felt. It didn't mean she was ready to get back together right away, but maybe they could start trying to talk again and then build up to something more. After her date with Steve it was obvious that the whole getting-over-Ken thing wasn't going to work. So why was she going to keep fighting it?

Maria opened the front door to her house and

felt relief wash over her. She was home—and this day was finally over.

"Maria? Is that you?" her mother called from the kitchen.

Maria followed the sound of her mom's voice and found her standing at the kitchen sink, finishing up the dinner dishes.

"Hi, Mom," she said, trying not to show how upset she was. She wasn't up for a big question-and-answer session on her love life with her mom. She really just wanted to go to bed and let this day be over. Well, maybe she'd call Elizabeth first.

"You had some phone calls while you were on your date," her mom said, drying her hands and turning toward her.

Liz, Maria thought. She must have gotten Maria's e-mail. Of course everything had changed since she'd sent it.

"Don't you want to know who they were from?" her mom prompted.

"Sure," Maria said, opening the fridge and grabbing a bottle of water.

"Ken called three times," her mom said, smiling.

Maria whirled around. Ken had called *three* times?

"What did he say?" Maria asked.

"Nothing much. He just sounded very anxious to

talk with you," her mom said. "He asked that you call him if you got in at a reasonable time. Did he know you were on a date with someone else? Because he sounded strained when he mentioned you getting in late."

"Yeah, he did know," she said.

Maria quickly looked up at the clock that hung over the sink. It was a quarter to eight. She still had time to call.

Forget tomorrow. She was going to call him tonight, before she lost her nerve. She was going to tell him that she cared before she went crazy thinking about it anymore.

The car ride home after the meeting with Mr. Nelson had been so quiet, Will had felt like he was at the library on a Friday night. They'd been home for hours now, but there had still been hardly a word uttered since they had left the SVH parking lot. Of course, when they pulled into the garage, Mr. Simmons made a comment about hoping Will would "think seriously" about what they'd discussed with Mr. Nelson. And at dinner his parents exchanged some small talk about work. But other than that, it was silent treatment all the way. It was as if his parents were punishing him for not knowing what the next twenty years of his life would bring.

Hadn't he already been through enough this year?

Will sighed, then switched on the television. He'd been flopped across the sofa in the living room since after dinner, trying to get some homework done. But he couldn't concentrate.

Of course, the first thing that came on the TV was a sports channel broadcasting a football game. Will hit the power button on the TV, and the picture disappeared. He didn't think he could stomach watching a football game right now.

In the kitchen he heard his mother washing their dinner dishes. His dad was already upstairs, probably reading in their bedroom like he always did at night. Will eyed the newspaper lying on the coffee table, opened to the sports page. Why were sports always in his face now? Everywhere he looked, he saw reminders of the world he'd been shut out of.

Will picked up the paper, glancing at the picture of some local kid with an amazing record of blocks. The paper used to be packed with stories on *him*. One of his favorite parts of having an awesome victory was opening up the paper the next day and reading about the game he'd helped his team win.

Suddenly Will felt an urge to see all those articles. He had a file of clippings of old newspaper stories about himself from the *Sweet Valley Tribune* stored in one of the cabinets under the bookshelves. He knew it would hurt to look at it, but he felt this sick pull—he wanted to remember just how big he'd been before his knee got ripped apart.

Will crossed over and opened up the cabinet, digging around for the file. He pulled it out and sat back down on the couch, putting the file down in front of him on the coffee table. First he picked up the clippings on top. These were the most recent stories. One of them was about his injury. Will noticed the date above the headline. He couldn't believe it had been less than two months since the injury. Two months since he had thought he was set for life. His future had seemed so certain—four years at Michigan, then the pros, he and Melissa would get married—"Looking at your old clippings, huh?" Mr. Simmons said, piercing Will's thoughts.

Will jerked up his head and saw his dad standing next to him, wearing his bathrobe and holding an empty mug in his hand. He'd probably been on his way to the kitchen.

"Yeah," Will said, glancing down at the overflowing file.

"There sure were a lot of them," his dad said, admiration clear in his voice. Mr. Simmons had never been totally behind Will's dreams of a professional football career. He'd always wanted his son to focus more on school. Still, he'd been proud of Will's achievements on the field. Now what did the man have to be proud of?

"You should arrange them in a scrapbook or an album," his dad suggested. "That old file's going to fall apart soon." He gave Will a smile, the first one all night.

"Well, I don't think there will be any more," Will said, unable to hold back the bitterness. "So if it hasn't fallen apart yet, it should be fine."

"Listen, Will," his dad said, sitting down next to him on the sofa. "I know this hasn't been an easy couple of months for you. That's understandable. It's hard to go from being glorified by the papers to being just like everyone else. That world is glamorous, and it's easy to get caught up in it. The world of athletes and great competitors. Once you're outside that circle, you just feel like a spectator in the stands."

Yeah, Will thought. Lately he'd felt like a spectator on his own life.

"Anyway," his dad continued. "We'll get it all figured out. You'll be okay." He gave him an awkward pat on the shoulder, then got up and walked toward the kitchen.

Will watched him disappear into the other room, then returned his gaze to the clippings. His own father didn't even know how to act around him. How much more pathetic could he be?

He shook his head, then started flipping through the news stories to find his favorite—the one about the homecoming game where he'd broken the El Carro record for yards passed in a single game. It was one of his best games, but he also loved the article because it was so well written. It made you feel like you were there, on the field, with the players.

Will wondered if he'd ever be back in that inner circle. After all, like his dad said, it was only occupied by players—which he would never be again, coaches—which he'd pretty much ruled out, and the reporters who wrote the stories.

Wait a minute, Will thought. *The reporters, the sports journalists. The guys on the sidelines, reporting the story and getting their bylines in the paper.*

They still got a little bit of the glory. More than coaches, at least. Will started to get an idea—the best one he'd had in months. He was a decent writer. Not great, but not terrible. And he definitely knew a lot about sports. Why couldn't he be like one of those sports journalists and write about the games?

After all, these guys have almost as exciting lives as some of the players, he thought. Some of the really good reporters, like for *Sports Illustrated* and some of the major sports magazines, even got to travel and cover the professional sports teams.

But the *Sweet Valley Tribune* was a good place to

get a start. He glanced down at the byline on the story about his injury. It was written by Ed Matthews. Wait—that was right. He'd forgotten that Ken's dad was a sportswriter. That was perfect! Things were definitely looking up.

Maria took the stairs leading to her room two at a time. She didn't want to lose her nerve before she got up to her bedroom.

When she reached her room, she kicked the door shut and grabbed the cordless phone on her night-stand. Her heart was beating ridiculously fast as she dialed the Matthews's number. She knew it by heart, but she felt like she hadn't dialed it in forever.

Her hand tightly clutched the phone as it started to ring. One, two, three rings . . .

"Hello?"

It was Ken.

"Hi, Ken. It's Maria," she said quickly, hoping she didn't sound too breathless. She still wanted him to sweat a little before she told him how she felt.

But at least they were on the same page now—he was calling to plead for her forgiveness or, at the very least, to try to make things better between them. And she was ready to listen.

"Hi, Maria," he answered.

Maria frowned. He sounded pretty distant for

someone who was about to beg for her to come back to him. But maybe that was just because he didn't know what to expect from her. After the scene at HOJ and what had happened in the hallway earlier, Ken wouldn't have a clue what was going on in her head right now.

"Hi, my mom said that you called," she prompted. She might as well let him say what he wanted before she gave him the response she knew he wanted.

"How was your night?" he asked.

"Um, okay," Maria replied. She certainly hadn't thought he'd ask about her date with Steve. And there wasn't a trace of jealousy in his voice either. What was his deal?

"Good, I'm glad," he said. "Listen, Maria. I didn't call you to bother you about getting back together. You're right—it's not a good idea."

Maria's jaw fell open in disbelief. He was giving up that quickly? He'd tried for less than twenty-four hours to get her back, and now he was forgetting the whole thing?

She swallowed, trying to figure out what to say.

Luckily Ken continued and she didn't have to speak. "I have a favor to ask," he said.

A favor? Maria sank down on her bed, the energy sucked out of her. *He wants to ask me for a favor?*

This was not going at all how she'd planned.

"I was hoping that you could meet me tomorrow sometime and help me with that history paper we have due," he said. "You know, we used to do all our studying together, and it's the only reason my grades have been decent so far this year. I, uh, I can't do it without you."

Maria frowned. What was he talking about? He'd written papers without her help. They'd barely even been speaking since they'd broken up! Why did he suddenly think he couldn't type another word without her?

It didn't even matter. What mattered was that now that she'd finally decided she was ready to try and work things out, the jerk didn't want to anymore. But there was no way she could let him know she was hurt. She had to prove she could be around him and not feel anything. Obviously it hadn't taken him too long to realize that he could do that, so she wasn't about to be the one who couldn't move on.

"Sure, I can help you with the paper tomorrow," she said. "What's your topic?"

"Presidential elections," he said. "Why some have been so close and if the electoral college is good or bad."

"Okay, no problem," she said. "We can get there early and do it before first period."

"Great. Thanks," Ken said. "And I'm sorry if I

acted a little crazy the past couple of days. I promise all we'll do is work on the paper. I am definitely done trying to get us back together."

"Um, good," Maria said, forcing a chipper tone even though she was blinking back tears. "So, I'll see you tomorrow morning at the library." She had to get off the phone before she cracked.

"Bye," Ken said, then hung up.

Maria threw herself back down on the bed and grabbed a pillow, clutching it to her chest. She stared up at the ceiling, trying not to freak out.

He was so infuriating! Maria couldn't believe she had thought they'd get back together. She had been ready to pour her heart out to him and forgive him for all the stupid things he'd done. At least she hadn't spoken first and made a fool of herself. She rolled over on her side, gripping the pillow tightly. Ken really hadn't changed at all.

Will Simmons

I think I need a really cool name to be a reporter. Will Simmons is just pretty plain. I could be Skip McCraken, Lance Robbins, Scoop Andrews. There are a ton of good names, and I'll need to come up with a good one before my first story hits the _Tribune_ and then goes right on to be reprinted in _Sports Illustrated_.

CHAPTER 8
Speaking of Trust

Maria gazed around the SVH library on Friday morning, surprised at how many other students were there, studying quietly. She'd thought the place would be empty at this hour. Maybe it was better if there were more people around, though. It would make it easier for her to keep herself together, knowing she had witnesses if she lost it.

Why had she agreed to this again? Suddenly Maria felt like she kept making decisions she regretted two seconds later. That wasn't like her. She liked to have her whole life planned out. Every detail.

And this certainly didn't fit into the plan. She was helping a guy with a huge ego who didn't deserve it at all, and she had her *own* assignment to work on plus her scene from *West Side Story* that she was set to perform today.

But here she was. She'd gotten to the library early, before they'd agreed to meet. She hadn't been able to sleep very well the night before. She just kept replaying their phone conversation in her head. How could she have been so wrong about what he was going to say?

She opened her notebook and glanced at her watch. If Ken was going to keep her waiting, she might as well read over her adaptation of the scene. She was really proud of what she had done in reworking it. She thought it was even more romantic and modern than it had been before. The character's voices sounded so real. Her teacher, Ms. Delaney, had given her a great tip for writing dialogue. She said the line out loud as she wrote it to make sure it would sound good coming from the actors.

"What are you working on?"

Maria snapped her notebook closed and glanced up. Ken stood behind her, looking over her shoulder. "Oh, hi," she said. She hadn't even heard him walk over. She was just glad she hadn't been doodling anything about him that he might have seen. Not that she ever doodled about him anyway. Not often, at least.

"It's just some stuff for drama class," she explained, keeping her voice down so she didn't bug the other students. "I have to read a scene I've adapted today in class," she said as she stuffed the notebook back in her bag.

"Well, good luck," Ken said, sitting down next to

her. "That's what I'll need to get through this paper. I'm just stuck on how to open this thing. Thanks for agreeing to help me."

"Sure," Maria said. "Let's take a look at what you've got."

Ken pulled his research material and some books out of his bag, leaning over to hand them to her.

Maria caught a whiff of his scent—an earthy mix of his soap and aftershave. She missed that smell. *Stop it,* Maria ordered herself. She turned her attention to the books Ken had pulled from his bag.

"I don't know why I thought a paper on close presidential elections was a good idea. I mean, there's plenty of stuff written about it already. Maybe that's why I feel like I don't have much to add," Ken said, gripping a pen.

"I think it's a great topic," Maria said. "No one ever thinks of the guys who lost years after the election. And some of the races were really close."

Ken grinned, and Maria felt her heart skip.

"You really like it?" he asked. Maria thought he moved his chair a little closer to her. She had to remind herself that he was probably just trying to see what she would write down to help him get started.

"You could start out with just naming the presidents who won by a narrow margin and then asking what they all have in common. Then launch into an explanation of how many people don't realize just how close some presidential elections actually were," Maria said.

"That's a great idea!" Ken said brightly.

"That's one way to open it up," Maria said. "I have another idea, though, that you could—"

"What's up, Matthews?"

Ken turned in the direction of the voice, and Maria followed his gaze. Todd Wilkins and what appeared to be the rest of the football team were standing near the book return.

"Shhh!" a girl sitting alone at a table hissed. She shot Ken a dirty look before returning to her book.

Maria couldn't believe it. She didn't think Todd Wilkins and those other football heads even knew where the library was, but there they were, bothering them. Did Ken tell them that he was going to be here? That was a dumb move.

"Whatcha working on?" Jason Rumsey asked in a loud whisper.

Ken flashed Maria an apologetic look, then got up. "I need to talk to them," he said. "I'll be right back."

Here we go again, Maria thought. Ken blowing her off for football. She was familiar with this routine.

Ken and the guys were standing nearby, and Maria couldn't help but listen in to their conversation.

"Hey, guys, I'm pretty busy right now. Can I catch you later?" she heard Ken say.

Maria's eyebrows shot up, and the corners of her mouth curled into a small smile. This was surprising. Ken finally had his priorities in order.

The paper—not her! After all, they weren't a couple anymore.

She picked up Ken's notebook so she could start writing down her ideas. The guys were still keeping him—probably urging him to leave and try a few plays before class.

But now that she knew Ken was serious about working on his paper instead, Maria wanted to help him. She opened his binder, and a bunch of stapled papers fell out of the notebook onto the floor.

Maria bent down to pick them up and quickly glanced at the title: "A Look at Our Nation's Closest Presidential Elections," by Ken Matthews.

As she flipped through, she started to feel sick. It was a completed draft of the very paper they were supposedly "working on"!

Maria couldn't believe it. How could he lie to her like that? Call her up and ask for help with a paper that he had already finished? Just when she'd thought he had changed too. She really was an idiot for falling for this. Finally it made sense—Ken hadn't been giving up on anything. He'd used this paper excuse as a way to spend time with her. Okay, yeah, there was a little twinge of happiness that he hadn't meant what he'd said about not wanting to get back together. But it didn't matter anymore. Because this whole scheme just made her see that her instincts were right and she couldn't trust Ken anymore.

Ken slapped some of the guys a high five as he walked back to the table. Maria's only regret was that they were in the library, where she—unlike the hulking football players—would have to keep her voice down.

"Ken, what is *this?*" she demanded in a stage whisper, holding up the paper.

Ken paled. He gulped and opened his mouth to speak, but Maria didn't need an explanation. What she needed was to tell Ken just how low he had gone.

"I can't believe you'd try to manipulate me like this. You've already done the paper!" she said, barely able to keep from yelling.

The girl at the next table who had shushed the football players turned around again to shoot Maria a matching glare. Maria just ignored her.

"Ken, I have an important scene for drama class that I could have been rehearsing, but instead I'm here helping you with a paper that you've already finished," she said. "You really haven't changed. Maybe you broke up with Melissa, but you're still as full of yourself as you were then."

Ken's eyes filled with pain—it was worse than she'd ever seen him look, even back when he was still mourning Olivia. It was like she'd ripped something right out of him. But maybe he needed that. He certainly needed *something* to help him see how out of control he was.

She packed up her books, throwing them inside her bag. This was getting to be a habit—her packing up her books and walking away from him. Unfortunately it didn't seem like it was one that would end anytime soon.

Jade entered the SVH main building on Friday morning with one thing on her mind—confronting Evan. She hadn't answered when he called last night because she had to do this in person. Jade had told Evan everything about her past—about Jeremy and the way she used to date around a lot. But Evan hadn't thought she deserved the same thing from him. She'd had to learn about how serious his feelings for Elizabeth were from Jessica. That was wrong, and she was going to get an explanation.

On top of that, she was going to make it crystal clear that he had a choice to make. He could keep on being Elizabeth's security blanket—her shoulder for when mean old Conner hurt her feelings—or he could be Jade's boyfriend. He couldn't be both.

If everything went the way she hoped, by the end of this talk he'd be begging her for forgiveness and they'd be busy setting up times for the movie they were going to see.

Jade smiled smugly as she strode through the hallway toward her locker. She had purposely taken a little longer getting ready this morning. She had worn her favorite vintage leather jacket and best-fitting jeans. She had even taken time picking out the perfect shade of deep burgundy lip gloss to top it off. If she was going to tell Evan how she felt, she wanted to look her best. She wanted him to realize that Jade was the only girl who really mattered to him.

She was unloading her books into her locker when she noticed the Polaroid picture of her and Evan that was hanging inside. They had been at a party and were smiling, with their faces pressed together. They made a great couple.

"Hey!" Evan said, peering around the side of her locker door and giving her a peck on the cheek.

Jade's breath caught. She closed her eyes as Evan's lips touched her face.

"Hey there, yourself," she said. She couldn't prevent herself from flirting with Evan, even though she was mad at him.

There was silence for a moment as Jade thought about how best to bring up what she had to say. She wanted to let him know that it was bothering her, but she knew how guys freaked at the direct-accusation thing. She had brushed up on her how-to-fight-right etiquette in a teen magazine last night. She wanted to see if the advice would work.

"Listen, Evan, can we talk?" Jade asked, closing her locker door and turning to face him.

"Sure," Evan replied. "Actually, I've been meaning to talk to you since you ran out of the cafeteria yesterday."

Jade's pulse quickened. Was he about to break up with her to get back together with Elizabeth? She couldn't believe this was happening. Elizabeth Wakefield had managed to ruin her relationship by butting in one too many times.

Suddenly Jade felt her cheeks flush. She could feel herself getting angry. She wanted to keep her cool, but she knew she couldn't.

She was more upset than she'd realized. That one little comment really set her off. Since *she* ran out of the cafeteria? How about, he wanted to apologize to her after running *her* out of the cafeteria?

"Well, I wouldn't have had to run out of there if you and Liz hadn't been having such a personal conversation in front of me," Jade snapped.

Uh-oh, Jade thought, cringing. *I need to calm down, or this is going to get ugly.* In her head she knew this wasn't the way to get him wrapped around her finger, where she wanted him. But somehow that knowledge wasn't penetrating to her mouth.

"What? Liz was just upset," he said.

"Yeah, for a change," Jade said. "Why are you so considerate with Elizabeth when what she did was so completely wrong?" She paused, then couldn't hold the next part back. "Is there still something going on with you guys?"

Evan's eyes opened wide, and his mouth hung open in shock. "What? No, of course not," he replied. "Listen, there's nothing between us anymore. I can't believe you'd think that."

"Why? She's only all over you when I'm sitting right there. What does she do when I'm not in the room?" Jade asked, her voice growing louder.

"Jade! Keep your voice down," he said. His eyes darted around the hallway, which was starting to fill.

He was right. A few people were looking over at them, obviously enjoying a free public scene. This school was so gossip hungry, it was pathetic.

"I don't care if people look," she said, glancing around.

"Well, I do," he said a little more softly. "Especially since this involves more people than just the two of us."

"I thought so," she burst out. "This isn't about us. You're trying to protect *her!*"

Evan touched her arm, but she shrugged it off.

"Jade, can we just go somewhere more private?" he pleaded. "How about one of these empty classrooms?" he said, pointing to an open doorway.

Jade shook her head. Evan needed to give her answers right now if he wanted to calm her down. She was getting snickers and stares from the people walking by, but Jade didn't care.

"I want to know what exactly happened between you and Liz while Conner was in rehab," she said. "Did you really only hook up once? Or were there other times?"

Out of the corner of her eye she saw a figure heading their way stop still in the middle of the hallway. She focused in on his features, and her heart sank. It couldn't be. But it was. And from the way his eyes were narrowing and his lips forming a thin, angry line—it was clear Conner had overheard everything she'd just said.

Jade's face paled, and she glanced back at Evan, her lower lip trembling. "Evan, I'm—I'm sorry."

Evan frowned in confusion, then slowly turned to see what Jade had been looking at behind him. When he looked back at Jade, there was something in his eyes she'd never seen before. That was because she'd obviously never seen Evan mad. His hands clenched into fists at his sides.

Jade's heart went all the way down to her toes. She'd messed up—big time. There was no way she could take it back now, though. Practically the whole school would hear about this by lunch. Of course, none of those people really mattered.

Only one person mattered. Conner, one of Evan's best friends, had heard her ask Evan just how many times Evan fooled around with Conner's girlfriend behind his back.

Jade didn't know what to say. But she couldn't take the way Evan was looking at her, and she really couldn't face Conner, who was now striding toward them. So she turned and took off down the hallway, realizing that she had just sent Evan and Elizabeth straight into each other's arms.

Conner watched, stunned, as Jade disappeared around the corner. He couldn't believe what he'd just heard. Elizabeth had hooked up with *Evan* while he was at rehab? How could Evan pull such a low move? He and Elizabeth might have been broken up, but Evan knew how much Elizabeth meant to Conner, whether they were officially together or not. And why did he have to learn this in the hallway in the middle of the school from some random girl he hardly knew? How come Evan hadn't told him the truth? How come *Elizabeth* hadn't?

It hit him that he wasn't sure he could control himself if he said anything to Evan right now. He needed to cool off—to think. Conner strode right by Evan, restraining himself from throwing a punch right there in the hall.

"Conner—wait!" Evan called out. "Wait a second."

Conner stopped and turned around slowly. Evan actually wanted to try to talk to him now after everything that had just happened? Didn't he know Conner a little better than that?

"What?" Conner bit out, the blood rushing through his veins.

Evan stared back at him blankly. So the guy wanted to talk, but he didn't have anything to say. That was a first for Evan. For any of Conner's friends, actually.

"I—um, I want to . . ." Evan's voice trailed off, and he just kept looking at Conner helplessly.

Conner took a couple of steps back toward Evan, carefully keeping a good distance between their bodies. "You want to try and explain what just happened?" he said. "How I somehow managed to hear you and your girlfriend talking about me and Liz in the middle of the hallway?"

"I'm sorry," Evan managed. "Really, man, I'm sorry."

Conner felt his lips curl into a mean half smile.

"I'll bet you are—now. Now that you've been caught," he said.

Evan flinched. "No, it's not that," he said. He walked over to the side of the hallway, and Conner followed. Conner wasn't up for a big scene any more than Evan was.

"I know what I did wasn't cool," Evan said once they were out of everyone's earshot. "But you have to remember that you two weren't together and I've known Liz for a while. I was into her even before you guys went out."

"News to me," Conner muttered. That was even better—his friend had been after his girlfriend all along. That made him feel really good.

"It wasn't like that," Evan argued. "I knew you guys had a thing, and I didn't want to get in the way, so I didn't say anything to you. But after you guys broke up, it seemed like you were over for good. You were the one who wanted that, Conner. At least, that's what Elizabeth said." He shifted his ratty backpack higher on his shoulder, the Greenpeace sticker coming into view. "Look, I acted like a real jerk," Evan admitted. "And I should have told you when you got back in town. But Elizabeth said she wanted to tell you herself, and I thought that made sense. This is really between you guys now, right?"

Something clicked in Conner's brain as he listened

to his friend. Elizabeth had been the one to say it should be kept a secret. Elizabeth had looked him in the eye, listened to him apologize about Alanna, and not said a word about her and Evan.

Evan was one of his best friends. This was low, but so was a lot of the stuff Conner had pulled before. And Evan had some decent points. Decent enough that Conner's body temperature had decreased considerably in the past twenty seconds.

Conner shrugged. "I know I was a jerk when I was drinking," he said. "And you just stood there and took it. You get points for that, and I can't just forget it." He took a deep breath. "Just don't hold out on me, man. You're one of the few people I can trust."

One of the very few, Conner thought. A part of him couldn't stop reeling over the idea that Elizabeth had betrayed him like that and still managed to act like the one being betrayed. He'd been so right about that girl the first time he ever saw her. She didn't belong in his world.

"Yeah, no more secrets," Evan said.

Conner nodded, then looked down at the floor. He still wanted to hit the guy when he pictured him kissing Elizabeth. But the urge wasn't as strong as it had been a few minutes ago. Actually, there was someone he was a lot more angry with right now.

"Speaking of trust," Conner said, running a hand

through his hair. "Elizabeth and I were broken up, yeah. She had as much of a right to—" He stopped, unable to complete the thought when that nasty image came back into his head. "She was as free as I was," he said instead. "But I *told* her about Alanna. And she managed to pull one of those classic I'm-so-perfect-but-I-love-you-anyway acts, making me feel like the dirt under her shoes. Like I should be grateful she wants me." Conner let out a harsh laugh. "What a load," he said.

"Conner—"

"I don't want to hear it," Conner cut him off. No one was going to convince him that he was the wrong one. Not anymore.

Jade Wu

Okay. The stupid-idiot-of-the-year award definitely goes to me. I was so intent on keeping Evan and Elizabeth apart that I made, like, the most obvious mistake in the world. I pushed him right at her by acting like a jealous freak. Even worse, I managed to make sure that Conner will probably never speak to Elizabeth again, leaving her free and clear for Evan. And even if Evan can get over the whole psychotic-girlfriend-making-a-public-scene thing, how's he supposed to forgive me for probably making one of his best friends hate him?

I had the whole thing planned so well in my head. I just completely lost it when Evan and I started talking. God, that means I really like him a lot. More than anyone else I've ever dated. What a great time for that to sink in.

CHAPTER 9
Turn Back the Clock

Ken looked up at the sky, glaring at the loud birds circling overhead. He'd never been so annoyed at the sounds of nature.

He had decided to eat his lunch alone, outside. Maria usually ate in the cafeteria, so this was a good way to avoid her disapproving stares.

It was another perfect southern California day. The stupid birds were chirping like crazy, and the sun shone down brightly. He had hoped this weather would make him feel better. But he really wasn't having much luck at reversing his mood. In fact, the brilliant weather only seemed to be making him feel worse.

Even the students surrounding him were bothering him. They were all acting so *happy*—chattering about upcoming weekend plans. It looked like he'd be spending Saturday night at home by himself while his dad was out on one of his many dates. Pretty pathetic that his own single father had a more interesting social life than he did.

The worst part of that scene with Maria in the library this morning was that it had made Ken wonder if he and Maria would even be friends again. She'd been annoyed at him all week, he knew. But today she seemed completely furious.

Why had he been such an idiot and left the finished paper in his notebook? Maybe Maria was right with all her stereotypes about dumb jocks. Todd's advice had certainly been no help. All it had done was get him in worse trouble with Maria than he'd been so far.

He had made so many mistakes in the past few days. First, the messed-up apology at House of Java, then the flirtation with another girl, then the asking-for-help routine. Strike three—he was definitely out.

Ken was seriously running out of options at this point. He could stake out her house and bar her entrance inside until she heard him out. That actually wasn't such a bad idea, considering how everything else had crashed and burned pretty badly.

Ken could hardly get down his hamburger, but he knew if he didn't eat something before practice, he was bound to have another bad afternoon with Coach Riley yelling at him. He didn't think he could stand another day of having both Maria hating him and Coach Riley criticizing his playing.

Still, if he had to choose—he'd take a million cuts from Coach Riley over losing Maria. *I just wish*

Maria got that, he thought, taking a small bite of his hamburger. That had been the first problem, right? Maria had actually believed that football was more important to Ken than she was. And maybe for a little while, it was. When he was first getting that position back, the excitement of being a star quarterback again was overwhelming. There wasn't room for much else, and he felt so much pressure to get back in shape and earn the trust of his teammates.

But he had football now, and he didn't have Maria. And how did he feel? Lousy. Much worse than when it was the other way around.

Maybe that's what I have to tell Maria, he realized, sitting up straighter. He'd been spending the past couple of days telling her he wanted her back, but she was right about what she said—he hadn't shown her that he'd changed at all. The truth was that she meant everything. He cared just as much about her drama scene as he did his history paper. In fact, he had even planned to ask her if he could read her drama scene when they had finished brainstorming for his paper. It actually sounded interesting, and Maria was such a good writer, he was sure she'd made the scene even better than the original. He could have given her some reassurance, told her she was going to do a great job. But now it was too late.

Or is it? Ken put down his hamburger. He couldn't

eat anymore anyway. But now he had something to distract him.

For the first time since this whole mess started, Ken had an idea that he was pretty sure could actually work. It was better than a confrontation, flirting with another girl, or pretending to need Maria's help. It was even better than telling her how he felt. He could show her. He could prove that what she thought was more important to him than anything anyone else thought. This would probably be the most embarrassing thing he'd ever done, but if it worked—then that was all that mattered.

Yes! There he is, Will thought as soon as he spotted Ken coming down the hallway. Will had been looking for him all day between classes and at lunch, but the guy was playing missing person or something.

He looks like he's in a hurry, Will realized, frowning. Ken was moving through the hall at a brisk pace, his face set in a determined expression as if he were on some kind of mission.

But Ken could make a little time for Will, the guy whose life he'd totally taken over, right? Will had to find out about Ken's dad and the sports department at the *Tribune.* If Will didn't talk to Ken right now, all the questions everyone had about his future just might make him break.

Will had been up half the night, trying to decide if he was kidding himself imagining he could be a sports reporter. There was only one way to find out for sure.

"Hey, Ken!" Will half shouted down the hall as Ken approached. It was hard for him to keep the urgency or the enthusiasm from his voice.

Ken stopped short. "Hi, Will," he said, letting Will catch up with him. "What's up?" he asked, glancing past Will in the direction where he'd been headed.

"Do you have a second?" Will asked, poised on his crutches.

"Uh, yeah, just a few minutes. I have to get somewhere," Ken said.

"That's fine," Will said. "I just wanted to ask you a couple of quick questions. See, I've been thinking lately about what I can do now that football is out of the question."

Ken cleared his throat, and his eyes shifted away. Will realized that Ken's guilt could definitely work to his advantage here.

"But I had a really good idea last night," Will continued. "I've decided I should try out sports journalism as a career. I noticed that your dad is the man at the *Tribune.*"

"Yeah, he is," Ken said. His tone was a little strange, but Will figured it was probably just from whatever Ken was in a rush to do.

"Do you think you could talk to your dad about helping me get a job at the paper?" Will asked. "I mean, not a full-time job, but maybe there's some kind of internship or something."

Ken's shoulders relaxed, and he smiled. *Good, I was right,* Will thought. Ken was relieved that he had the chance to help Will. Will knew that if the situation were reversed, he'd feel bad enough to do just about anything for Ken.

"That's a great idea, man," Ken said. "Writing for the sports section would be perfect for you. You already come to all the games, and you definitely know the lingo."

"Yeah, a little too well," Will said. "Coach Riley sure drills it all into your head when he's yelling about everything you did wrong."

Ken laughed. "Tell me about it," he agreed.

This is pretty cool, Will thought. Things had been rough between him and Ken for a while. The quarterback position and then the thing with Melissa had really sent Will over the edge for revenge. But now things were better, and it looked like Will had made an important ally.

"I'll talk to my dad this weekend and let you know what he said on Monday," Ken said. He glanced down at his watch, the anxious glint returning to his eyes.

"Great! Thanks, man," Will said. "I'll let you go

now. You look like you have something important to take care of."

"Yeah, I do," Ken said. "See you later." He took off again at an even faster speed than he'd been walking before they talked.

That couldn't have gone better, Will thought as he strolled down the hall. He was pretty satisfied that his new dream was going to come true.

It was just going to take some patience and determination, but football had taught him both of those things. A career as a journalist would be awesome and exciting, and he could do it for a long time. A football player only had like ten or fifteen good years as a pro before retiring. This way he could be set permanently.

It was like a huge weight had been lifted from his shoulders. Maybe senior year might turn out okay after all. He was tempted to knock on Mr. Nelson's door and tell him not to worry about him anymore. Will Simmons was going to be just fine. Coach Riley might be disappointed that he wasn't going to be a coach, but Will knew he'd be happy for him too. His parents sure had liked the idea.

Best of all, Melissa would have to be impressed with the idea of him becoming a sportswriter. He wasn't planning on sticking with some dinky paper like the *Tribune* for long. He'd be at *Sports Illustrated* or something even bigger. Maybe he'd even get into

TV work. Melissa would *love* that. He couldn't wait to tell her his news.

Jade looked around the cafeteria at all the tables full of friends eating together, then glanced back down at her tray. Two days ago Evan would have been sitting here with her, lecturing her for ordering meat and stealing her potato chips on the sly. But now it was just her, eating all by herself. Not that she was eating very much. She couldn't stomach any food.

What had gotten into her this morning? Why hadn't she just kept her mouth shut or agreed to talk later or gone into an empty classroom like Evan had suggested? She bit her lip. She had never come so close to crying in school. Even now she could feel the lump forming in her throat.

Jade was just about to get up and leave when she spotted Evan walking over to her. She met his gaze for a second, trying to read his expression, but then quickly looked back down at her food, afraid to see whatever was in his eyes.

"Hey," he said, taking a seat across from her.

"Hey," she said, still focusing on her hot dog. "So I guess you're talking to me."

"Yeah," Evan said. "I am. But it doesn't mean I'm not mad. What was with that scene you pulled this morning? Do you have any idea how angry Conner was?"

Jade winced. "I was angry too," she said softly. "I know that sounds lame, but I really don't have an excuse." She raised her eyes slowly, relieved to see that he didn't look anything like the way he did in the hall this morning. The familiar openness was back in his warm brown eyes, and she realized that maybe she had a chance here.

Please don't stay mad at me, Jade tried to convey with her best pleading look.

"Okay, you were upset," Evan said. "I get that. I should have filled you in more on me and Liz, and I shouldn't have made you feel like I was ignoring you for her problems. But why did you have to raise your voice so loud and refuse to talk about it in private?" he asked. "You knew that Liz wanted to tell Conner what happened with us herself. Why couldn't you keep things quiet until she had the chance to tell him?"

Jade pushed the food around on her plate. Her hot dog looked like rubber and was probably just as cold. Her baked beans had congealed. This food looked about as bad as she felt right now.

Why couldn't she turn back the clock to yesterday and start over? All she really needed was to relive the past twenty-four hours and make everything right.

She shrugged. "I never thought that Conner would hear us," she said. "It's a big school, you know? What were the chances that he'd be walking up right at that moment? It was just bad luck."

Evan glanced around the cafeteria. Jade wondered if he was checking to see if Conner might surprise them again. Or if he was hoping to see Elizabeth.

"What happened after I left?" she asked.

"Well, he finally calmed down a little," Evan said. "With me, at least. But he's *really* mad at Liz for not telling him, and I don't know if he's ever going to let her off the hook." The anger was creeping back into his voice.

Big surprise. Again Evan's concern for his precious Elizabeth meant more than how he felt about Jade.

"That's exactly why I was so upset, Evan," Jade burst out. "I'm pretty sick of feeling like number two. You obviously care more about Elizabeth than you do about me."

Evan squinted at her like she'd just said something he couldn't even understand. "Are you serious?" he said. "You actually think that?"

"Well, every time I'm around and she's here too, you seem to magically forget my existence. And right now you're not even mad because I upset Conner or caused problems between you guys. You're mad because I did something to get Princess Elizabeth in trouble."

Evan shook his head, his long, black hair swinging back and forth. "I was just trying to be a good friend to her," he said. "She's been through a lot, and

I wanted to be there for her." He stopped, leaning across the table. "And yeah, I'm not too happy with what she's in for now. Because she's *my friend.* Why is that so tough for you to understand?"

Jade gulped. Here she was again—sounding like the jealous nutcase. But she wasn't—she had a right to her fears. "But you've hooked up," she argued. "You weren't always just good buddies. And the way Jessica put it, you were practically obsessed with the girl. Am I really supposed to believe that's all over now?"

Evan sighed, pushing a few strands of hair back behind his ear. "Jade, my concern for Liz has absolutely nothing to do with the fact that I *used* to have feelings for her," he said.

Jade narrowed her eyes, studying his expression. He really seemed to be telling the truth. *And he said "used,"* she thought. *Used* to have feelings for her.

"I'm over Liz," Evan continued. "You're the one I wanted to be with. I was happier with you than I've been with anyone—including Elizabeth."

Jade felt a blast of excitement rush through her. No one had ever said anything like that to her. She knew Evan said what he meant too. She loved that about him. So if he said he wanted her, then he really wanted *her.* It was so amazing, she could barely keep from leaping up and grabbing him. But now she had to apologize for the mistakes she'd made and hope that Evan could forgive her. This time she was going to be as honest and direct as she could be. No more pretending.

"Evan, I promise I won't do anything like this again," she said, the words spilling out. She leaned forward eagerly. "Just say you forgive me, and we'll forget about all of this. Because I feel the same way. I do. You make me so—"

"I said I was happier with you," Evan said flatly. "And I was. At least, until all of this happened."

Jade froze. She licked her lips, not wanting to hear what he was saying. This couldn't be happening. The perfect guy had just told her that she was the one he wanted, and there was no way that two seconds later he would snatch that back from her. It was too cruel.

"Listen, I'm really not sure what's going to happen with us, Jade," Evan went on. "I think I just need a little space right now to think things over."

Jade's voice caught in her throat. All she could do was nod. The tears pressed against the backs of her eyelids, and she blinked them away.

How dense could she have been? Evan had liked her all along. Her! And she was so busy trying to find something wrong with it that she had probably ruined what they had for good.

"We'll see what happens," Evan said. He stood awkwardly, stuffing his hands in the pockets of his khaki cargo pants. "I'm sorry, but I just can't deal with this now." He turned and walked away, and Jade watched him go, fighting the urge to chase after him and beg. She still had a shred of pride left, and she wasn't going to lose it.

We'll see what happens. Please. Jade wasn't stupid. She knew what that meant. She and Evan were through—and it was all her fault.

To: jess1@cal.rr.com
From: jadewu@cal.rr.com
Subject: Help!

Hey, Jess.

So, I messed up big time. Things with me and Evan are pretty bad, and I don't know if they're going to get better. I know you're his friend . . . do you think you could convince him to give me another chance? You know me. I wouldn't be asking—especially you of all people—if I didn't really like him.

To: jadewu@cal.rr.com
From: jess1@cal.rr.com
Subject: re: Help!

Hey, Jade,

I'm sorry things didn't work out. I can try to help, but Evan's pretty stubborn. He doesn't really listen to me. I know honesty's a huge thing with him. Just try to tell him what you really feel. . . . Good luck!

Jess

Conner McDermott

I haven't gotten to talk to Liz in school today. Probably better. I'm not really up for another big scene. So I'll just get through creative writing without looking her in the eye, let the day end, and then catch up with her tonight.

Because this can't wait much longer. I've finally made a decision, and now I know exactly what I need to do. All that's left is doing it.

CHAPTER 10
Following Our Hearts

Concentrate, Maria told herself as she walked to drama class. *I just need to get through the rest of the afternoon, and then I can have all weekend to wallow in self-pity over Ken.*

Her head was still reeling from what had happened in the library before school. She'd been a mess all day. She'd have to get the notes from people in her classes. But she needed to pull herself together for her drama scene. This was like twenty percent of her grade, and she had put way too much time and energy into it to let it be ruined by a run-in with Ken.

Maria entered the theater and started jogging down the steps. She looked around to see if Jessica and Tia were here yet, then stopped dead in her tracks, unable to believe what she was seeing.

Ken was sitting in the front row.

What is he doing here? The guy had become a stalker—a stalker trying to ruin her life!

Ken looked up at her and gave her a small smile.

For a second he reminded her of the old sweet, shy Ken. But then she remembered that he was sitting here in her class. Maria shook her head, then glanced away from him and walked over to a seat on the opposite section. First he lied about his paper and took away from time she needed to work on her scene. Now here he was in her drama class. What was he thinking?

"Class, we have a special guest actor here today to act out one of your classmate's scenes," Ms. Delaney said, giving Maria a mysterious smile. "While the rest of you will call on one another to read other characters in your scenes, he has asked to join the writer for her adaptation of a scene from *West Side Story.* Ken, Maria, why don't you come up to the stage?"

Ken was already on his feet, standing awkwardly before the class, his face a shade paler than usual.

Maria felt the eyes of everyone in the room boring holes into her. She started to object. She wanted to say that she had intended to call on someone else to play the part of Tony, but Ken looked so nervous standing up there. Nervous and vulnerable.

He was ready to try something he had never done before in front of a roomful of people. *This is definitely not an egomaniac move,* she realized, seeing the fear in his blue eyes. Ken hated reading aloud—even when it was just the two of them alone together. And he definitely wasn't an actor. He'd always told her he couldn't believe she was able to get up and act in front of people, that he'd be way too scared.

Maria stood and headed for the stage to join him, clutching the two copies of the scene in her hand. As she got closer, she noticed that his hands were trembling slightly under the stage lights. The guy was seriously freaked. She was afraid to let herself even think it . . . but it was hard to avoid. This was the Ken she knew, the Ken she'd fallen for. He was putting her first—about to do something that terrified him just to prove he cared.

She gave him a small, reassuring smile. If he was ready and willing to do this, then so was she.

"I've chosen to adapt a love scene between Maria and Tony from *West Side Story*," Maria explained to the rest of the class. She caught Tia's eye, and Tia grinned back at her, then winked. "Everyone knows the story pretty well already," she went on, trying not to blush. "So I guess you don't need too much background. I updated some of the language and tried to make it more believable and modern. I hope you like it."

Maria handed Ken his copy of the scene, and he swallowed hard. The first line was his, and she waited for him to start.

"Maria, I had to come here to apologize to you," he said stiffly, staring at the page. He gripped the corners of the papers tightly.

"Tony, you'd better leave," Maria said, letting her voice take on the urgency of the character's. "My brother will kill you if he finds out that you're here."

"I don't care. I really don't care. I realized that tonight. When I saw you at the dance. I—I think I'm in love with you." Ken looked up from the paper, and Maria's throat got tight as she saw all the genuine emotion in his eyes despite his awkward recitation of the lines.

"We are way too different for this to ever work out," Maria said, turning her attention from Ken back to the scene. "We come from two totally different worlds."

"But isn't that what makes us interesting? That we're not alike. That we *are* from two different worlds?" Ken asked, his voice cracking. He moved closer to Maria and looked her in the eye.

For a moment Maria's breath caught. She hadn't even realized how closely this scene mirrored their situation. Maybe subconsciously that's why she'd chosen to adapt it.

"But what about our families and friends? We might not have anyone else's support in this," she said. Her voice was shaking slightly, and suddenly everything else in the room seemed very far away.

"As long as we have each other, I think that's all that's important," Ken said.

"But is it all that's important, Tony?" Maria asked, her voice getting stronger. She stood up straight and really felt the words she said. "We live in a world that judges us pretty harshly. We're supposed to hang out with people who are like us. Jocks hang out with jocks. Brains hang out with brains. Band members hang out with other people in band."

"If that were true all the time, it sure would be boring," Ken said, giving her a wink.

Maria could feel the blood rise to her face. Ken had changed the line, but it worked perfectly.

"So, what you're saying is that we shouldn't care about what anyone else thinks? Just follow our hearts?" Maria asked. Her own heart was racing, and she wiped her sweaty palm on her jeans.

"Just follow our hearts, and make sure we never stop showing each other how much we care. Everything else will fall into place," he said.

Maria had lost her place in the scene, but it didn't matter. She had a feeling that Ken was really speaking as Ken, not Tony, and he was speaking from his heart, not reading off the page.

"I love you," he said, touching her arm. Electric shivers traveled down her spine.

"I love you too," she said, looking up at him.

He stepped closer and wrapped his arms around her, pulling her to him. And then, suddenly, he was leaning down to kiss her. For the briefest moment his lips met hers in a kiss she could feel all the way down to her toes, and then he pulled back. But as quick as the kiss was, the moment seemed to freeze, and a million thoughts rushed through Maria's head. Over everything else was one, clear feeling—overwhelming happiness.

The class was silent for a moment, not sure whether this was part of the scene and they were witnessing some great acting or whether what they were watching was real. A very personal moment between two real people, not characters in a scene.

Someone started clapping, and the entire class caught on. Maria glanced back at the audience, blushing like crazy. Her eyes darted over to Ms. Delaney as it hit her that she'd just kissed Ken in front of her *teacher*. But Ms. Delaney was smiling and clapping along with all the students. Maria remembered that she'd been the one to let Ken do this. Obviously her old drama teacher didn't mind one little break from the normal school rules.

Ken squeezed her hand, and they both took their bows. Maria blinked, wondering if she was dreaming. But this was real—and it was perfect. She and Ken were back together. And she had a feeling that this time, it was for good.

Will hadn't felt this good since running a winning play on the football field. Talking with Ken had made him feel like he actually had a future to look forward to.

The only problem was that he hadn't seen Melissa yet. He really couldn't wait to share his good news. It almost felt like it wasn't real until he got to tell her about it.

He already had the timeline worked out in his head. He was going to work for the *Tribune* next semester and hopefully over the summer. Then he'd go to college, maybe somewhere local if he couldn't get into Michigan. That way he could continue at the *Tribune* and get more experience. Then, after he graduated, he would get a job offer in Los Angeles for one of the big papers—or maybe something in New York. A magazine. And then? It was straight to television from there. His face would be more famous than most of the players' faces.

Yes, this was going to work out better than he could have ever imagined. It was already a great news story. *Star athlete doesn't realize his true calling in life until an injury sidelines him. Forced to rethink his future, he finds what he was meant to do instead.*

Will stopped at the vending machines near the cafeteria and put in some change. Melissa had to pass by here to get to cheerleading practice, so it was a good place to hang out. He pushed the button for a fruit juice, then spotted Melissa a second later coming his way.

"Liss, hey," he said. He grabbed the juice out of the machine and balanced on his crutches, heading toward her.

"Hi!" she said brightly. "How did it go yesterday?" She frowned. "You never called back—did you get my message?"

"Yeah, sorry," he said. "I was slammed with work." Actually, he just hadn't wanted to have to tell her the whole thing had been a total failure. But he didn't have that problem anymore. "The meeting wasn't so good," he said. "But then later I got a great idea for what I can do."

"Good," she said, smiling "But you're not going to be a coach, right?" she added, her eyes narrowing.

"No way," he said. "You were definitely right about that. No, I have something much better. Since I can't play football, I'm going to write about it. I'll still get to go to all the big games and be right in the center of the action. I'll be the one to make or break the players' careers." He grinned at her, knowing just how to get her as excited as he was. "It's major power, Liss," he said.

Her eyes lit up. "Will, that's excellent," she said. She paused, wrinkling her nose. "But you don't mean, like, a writer for the Sweet Valley paper, right?"

Will laughed. This was why he and Melissa belonged together. Their minds worked in sync.

"Yeah, well, I'll have to start out pretty small," he said. "But then I'll work my way up. I figure if I start now, then after college I should have my pick of some really top newspapers and sports magazines.

And then I'll slide right into the televised stuff."

"I can see you as a famous sportscaster already," Melissa said, stepping closer to him. She traced her fingers along his arm. "I told you, Will," she said. "You and I are going to be right back on top soon. Together. Where we belong."

Elizabeth couldn't believe her luck. Another Friday night and she was working again. Why was she always down on the schedule on nights when her friends were out having a good time? She'd have to talk to Carolee about changing her schedule. After all, with Conner back there was even a chance that soon she'd have actual *important* plans for the weekend.

Tonight was the worst too. She was stuck restocking the perfume counter. She was getting a headache from all the different smells leaking out of the bottles. She'd have to take a shower tonight, or her entire bed was going to smell like a flower garden had exploded in it.

At least the mall was pretty slow for a Friday. And keeping busy with the perfume helped a little with distracting her from wondering if Conner really had been avoiding her after creative-writing class today or if he'd just been in a hurry to get somewhere afterward.

She opened another box full of perfumes. Whew! She was never going to wear the stuff again. Even her favorite scent was making her feel queasy when she had to smell it at twenty times the normal strength.

She pushed a stray blond hair out of her face, scanning the counter. Why did it seem like she was the only one actually working? Tanya and Amber were gabbing about the latest nail colors to arrive, and Lisa was on a break.

Out of the corner of her eye she saw someone approach the counter. Finally, a customer to pull her away from the perfume.

She moved the bottles aside and glanced up, putting on her pleasant how-can-I-help-you? smile.

But the smile froze when she saw who was coming. It wasn't a customer. At least, not unless Conner had suddenly developed a strong interest in women's cosmetics.

Elizabeth's pulse immediately shot up. Conner was here. He had come here looking for her. So he'd made a choice—and it had to be her, right? Conner hated confrontations. If he didn't want to be with her, he would have blurted it out in the hall and then rushed away or maybe even said it on the phone or something. He wouldn't have come all the way to her job at a mall—one of his least-favorite places to be—unless he was ready to say he wanted her back as much as she wanted him back.

But as Conner got closer, she began to sense that something was wrong. His mouth was set in a line, and his eyebrows were furrowed. He got all the way up to the counter without a hint of a smile or any kind of greeting.

"I can't believe you," he said, his voice so low, she could barely hear it.

Elizabeth jerked back. "What—What are you talking about?" she asked, swallowing hard.

"We both messed up, Elizabeth. Only I came clean about what I did. I told you about Alanna."

Elizabeth felt her stomach twist. He knew about Evan. He had to.

"What do you mean, we both messed up?" she asked, her mouth dry.

Conner shook his head. "You're still trying to pull this act," he said. "Elizabeth the sweet and perfect, and Conner the bad guy. Liz, drop it. I know about you and Evan."

Elizabeth took a shaky breath. "Conner, let me just explain," she started.

"Actually, no," he said. "I don't want to hear it."

Elizabeth licked her lips. What did she say to that? Conner was right. She should have told him about her and Evan. But she was planning to tell him—eventually. It just hadn't seemed like the right time ever. Couldn't he give her a chance to explain things, though?

Her eyes started to fill with tears. "Conner, I lo—"

"Liz, it's over," he cut in. "We're done. I'm sick of trying to be as perfect as you are. Especially when you're not, and you just can't accept it. We're wrong for each other. We've always been wrong for each other. So that's it, okay?"

He stared at her for a second, but her tongue was too thick to get a word out. She felt like she'd just been kicked in every inch of her body, and she didn't know how to recover.

"Good-bye, Liz," he said. And then he turned and walked away.

Conner slammed the door to his house shut behind him. Where had he put Alanna's phone number? Suddenly he felt like he couldn't wait another second to call her.

He pictured Alanna's soft, gray eyes and remembered the way it felt to kiss her. Everything between them had been easy, natural. Right. And everything with Elizabeth had always been just the opposite.

At least he finally knew it, though. Not just in his head, but in his gut. He knew that he didn't want to be with Elizabeth. Yeah, they had some kind of crazy connection. And for a while it had been good. But underneath that there was this gaping space between who he was and who she was.

Unlike with Alanna. They fit like he'd never fit with anyone. And Alanna gave it to him straight—she didn't hide things from him because she was afraid they wouldn't work with some perfect little image she wanted him to see. He knew all the ugly stuff, just like she knew those sides of him.

He went into the kitchen and turned on the light, then checked the fridge and the pad of paper near the phone. He knew that Alanna had called earlier in the week and she'd left her number. So where was it?

I can't believe I almost went back to Liz, he thought as he kept searching. He'd been right about that whole addiction thing. Elizabeth was an addiction, and at least finding out about her and Evan had helped him get it out of his system.

Conner left the kitchen and headed upstairs to his room, hoping his mom had left the number somewhere in there. He turned on his lamp on his desk and checked a pile of papers on the floor. He shoved some clothing off his chair and sat down at his desk.

The slip of paper with Alanna's name and number was lying right in front of him. He grabbed it, then reached for the phone and quickly dialed the number.

"Hello?" a female voice answered.

"Hi. Alanna?"

There was a pause. "Conner?" she said, her voice unsure.

"Yeah, it's me," he said. "And I've made my choice."

WILL SIMMONS

9:20 P.M.

Will Simmons was your typical star quarterback. He managed to take his team to victory nine times out of ten, he was dating a cheerleader, and he was being scouted by some of the top division-I college teams. He thought his life was pretty much perfect and nothing could bring him down.

But when an injury on the football field left him unable to play, he lost both his girlfriend and his scholarship, and he wasn't even sure he had a future anymore.

Until he learned that he could still be involved in the world of sports—if only from the sidelines. He was going to become a star reporter.

I've definitely got it. Now all I have to do is make it all happen.

KEN MATTHEWS

9:29 P.M.

My life is finally back on track and pretty much perfect. If I can just take the team to the championships and nail that scholarship to the University of Michigan, I'll have everything I want. Want, not need. Because now that I have Maria back, I already have everything I need.

ALANNA FELDMAN

10:37 P.M.

Conner chose me. Me. He said we belong together, and he always knew it. I know it too. I just wonder if he'd still feel that way if he knew everything about me. Maybe I shouldn't have kept stuff from him. But I think it's a little too late to let the truth out now. . . .